PRINCES

S O N Y A
H A R T N E T T

P R I N C E S

VIKING

VIKING
Published by the Penguin Group
Penguin Putnam Inc., 375 Hudson Street, New York, New York 10014, U.S.A.
Penguin Books Ltd, 27 Wrights Lane, London W8 5TZ, England
Penguin Books Australia Ltd, Ringwood, Victoria, Australia
Penguin Books Canada Ltd, 10 Alcorn Avenue, Toronto, Ontario, Canada M4V 3B2
Penguin Books (N. Z.) Ltd, Cnr Rosedale and Airborne Roads, Albany, New Zealand

Penguin Books Ltd, Registered Offices: Harmondsworth, Middlesex, England

First published by Penguin Books Australia, 1997
Published in the U.S.A by Viking, a member of Penguin Putnam Inc., 1998
1 3 5 7 9 10 8 6 4 2
Copyright © Sonya Hartnett, 1997
All rights reserved

Library of Congress Catalog Card Number: 97-60742
ISBN 0-670-87487-6

Designed by Ellie Exarchos, Penguin Design Studio
Typeset in 11.5/15 Weiss by Midland Typesetters, Maryborough, Vic.
Made and printed in Australia by Australian Print Group

The epigraph opposite comes from the *Satires* of Horace (II. iii. 243).

Par nobile fratrum
A noble pair of brothers

For Lucy

The author wishes to thank Geoffrey C. Ingleton
for permission to reproduce and adapt material
from *True Patriots All*, edited by Mr. Ingleton and
published by Angus & Robertson in 1952.

CONTENTS

THE RAVAGES OF SWINE

At the sound of the door closing, the dull dropping of the slabbed lock, the young pig opened its eyes. It had been dreaming, skimming through a bright and groundless world. Now it looked around the dark hut, arching its snout off the floor. Its soft ears – ears already shaped similar to the gloves they might one day become – detected more than did the silvery eyes, gummy from sleep, irritated by infected lashes. The blunt nose, most valuable appendage of all, sifted the smell of the woman. The woman was a towering and dangerous force in the life of the young pig. She consisted of legs, and booted feet. She had entered, and left, the room, pulling the door closed after her. The piglet was locked in the hut. It had been locked in the hut all morning, its white body wedged amongst the cooking pans beside the fireplace where the bricks gave off waves of self-contained warmth and the fragrance of eaten meals. The snub nose wavered, seeking the curious creature that now shared this private place. The sticky eyes succeeded in prising themselves open and the young pig rose to the extent of its short but able legs,

1

nodded its head sagely, and stepped out, spilling pots and pans.

————

The pig was domesticated by the Chinese some time around 3000 BC. The pig reaches maturity and reproduces its kind more quickly than does any other meat-producing animal. It can be eaten as pork, or as ham and bacon if the meat is cured. Parts of it – the head and trotters in particular – are considered delicacies. Even its scraps are not scraps: swine intestines are used as sausage casings, and its fat is poor-man's butter, lard. Its hide becomes expensive pigskin leather after it is tanned, and its hair is made to serve as bristles for paintbrushes. It is a cheap and easy animal to keep, being an eater of simple refuse. For all these reasons, pigs had reached such population that they had achieved the status of pest in the streets of Sydney in AD 1806. They were often found rummaging in the cemetery.

A pig is cloven-hoofed, thick-skinned, sparsely dusted with wiry hair. Pigs are clean animals, by nature: they coat themselves in cooling mud, when they must, in order to keep their skin protected from the sun. They are peaceful and enduring when left to their own devices, but they are wilful, stubborn, strong, lightning-quick and slick as glass when they oppose the intentions of others. They are omnivorous, as a scavenger should be, and their neat mouths contain forty-four teeth.

————

The piglet looked around the darkened hut, snout raised like a mast, busily sniffing. It was hungry: its hours of accidental imprisonment had been long, and detrimental to a fast-growing beast. It located what it sought by employing its eyes, its ears, its sense of smell. It stepped across the floor and paused briefly before the challenge that faced it, that of hauling its long, unathletic body onto a surface that was high, too high for the animal to inspect from where it stood. But it trusted the instincts which promised that what it wanted was indeed up there, reached with effort, but effort rewarded. The young pig reared clumsily, placing its trotters on the surface. It scrabbled with its back legs, sometimes finding purchase, sometimes flailing the air. It snorted, its eyes rolled, it fell, it tried again. It whimpered, afraid it would fail, and its stomach writhed. Its stomach was alive with worms, for the piglet often indulged in meals that were uncooked and unhealthy, and these worms were hungry too. The animal clambered up eventually, and shook itself vigorously, as if to cast off the memory of such demanding determination. This done, it set about eating.

When Sarah Pearce, she of the towering legs and booted feet, returned to the hut some minutes later, she found that the piglet had consumed the face and the left hand of the infant she had left sleeping on the pallet, and was in the absorbing process of devouring the right arm.

⎯⎯

Indigo Kesby sat back on his haunches, much pleased with this story. His brother looked at him in silence from where he, too, sat cross-legged on the floor. The brothers wore silk boxer shorts, and nothing else: Indigo's were burgundy, Ravel's olive-green. The room was lit by candles, as the electricity had been cut long ago. It was well past midnight and the brothers were glimmering in the candlelight because the night, like the day, was hot. Between them lay a plate on which Ravel had poured out spicy biscuits, one of which he now placed flat upon his tongue, feeling the spicing tingle.

'*Shame on the indecent miscreant!*' Indigo intoned, once more reading from the book. '*If detection alight upon his contemptuous crime he shall be shunned and pointed at.*'

3

'What's that?'

'Shunned and pointed at,' Indigo repeated. This was punishment in 1806 Sydney for letting your swine roam the cemetery. Shunned and pointed at.

Ravel spoke around the softening biscuit. 'What happened to it? Does it say what happened to it?'

'It got eaten.'

'Eaten, with a baby inside?'

'No, the baby got eaten.'

'The baby got eaten, yes –'

'Pig got forty-four teeth,' Indigo chortled, and rocked on his ankles. Ravel pressed the sodden biscuit to the roof of his mouth.

'What happened to the pig, is what I mean.'

Indigo frowned at the book in his lap. The heat had made his hair stringy, and curls of it stuck to his throat. He reached out a hand blindly as he read, knocking biscuits over the rim of the plate until his fingers fastened around one and delivered it, unseen, to his mouth.

'Maybe it got eaten, too,' Ravel suggested, as the moments went by.

'You don't eat a pig that's got your baby inside it,' his brother answered tersely. Indigo's moods came and went. He did not like being interrupted. Ravel watched the black eyes scan the page, squinting against the darkness, as if a narrower view would somehow help.

The voracious animal was shot immediately that the accident was discovered, and was afterwards burnt by the order of the Coroner.

'Voracious,' Ravel mused. He licked his teeth clean of biscuit remains. His brother closed the book and folded it to his chest. He propped his chin on the corner of the spine. Ravel looked at him.

'It was a good story.'

4

'It was a great story. I'm surprised you didn't find it first. Many points to me.'

'Ten.'

'Twenty, I think.'

Ravel didn't argue: they never added up the score.

'It's your turn now.'

Ravel extended his hand, but Indigo did not pass the book across the floor. He continued to sit, rocking slightly, his arms protecting the book and its tales. Ravel, after a moment, let his hand fall resignedly to the carpet which, like their shorts, was silk. They were surrounded by and accustomed to grandeur. Ravel flexed one finger and then another, feeling the bones and muscles work. 'It's hot,' he sighed.

'You won't sleep.'

'No. It's hot.'

'Another story, then.'

Still Indigo did not relinquish the book. Ravel continued to flex his fingers. Sweat travelled ponderously down their faces, more quickly down their chests and backs, droplets glorified by grace of golden candlelight until they soaked without ceremony into the elastic waists of boxer shorts. The air seemed thin. In a corner sat two watching rats, ash-coloured and as still as stone. Ravel wanted another biscuit, did not want another biscuit. He rapped his knuckles on the carpet. Still Indigo kept the book.

'Dastard must be the man that would thus pollute the mansions of the dead for such trifling gain.'

'Give me the book.'

'No.'

'I won't sleep.'

'Dastard be the man.'

'Indigo . . .'

'The mansions of the dead.'

Indigo looked into his brother's weary face.

'Look at you,' he said. 'My handsome twin.'

'The book, Indi –'

Indigo relented, and slid the book across the floor.

———

Multiple births are relatively uncommon amongst the larger mammals, and the tendency to produce more than one baby from a single pregnancy seems to be, in these uncommon animals, hereditary. The arrival of twins is the end result of around one in every ninety human pregnancies, and identical twins account for about 25% of all twin births. Identical twinship comes about when a single fertilised ovum splits into two, and two babies thus begin to grow. It is not only the womb that identical twins share; they will be the same sex, they will have similar blood types and fingerprints, and they will look almost indistinguishably alike. The twins will be strikingly similar, in every physical aspect, for the length of their lives – except during these nine important formative months, when it is not unusual for one twin to grow larger, heavier, and stronger, than the other. This bully twin sucks the choicest nutrients from the solitary placenta, leaving just leftovers for its weaker sibling. Side by side they lie in the womb, the boss twin, the little twin, waiting to be born. When they are, they face a higher mortality rate than do babies of single births.

The parents of our twins, Indigo and Ravel, were Kasbah and Annie Kesby. Were? Are. A parent does not become a parent in the past tense, but for all time. Parentage is not nullified by history. From Kasbah the twins get their fine unfreckled skin, the colour of dust-storms. From him comes their jet hair with its lazy curls and their deeply coloured eyes. Kasbah is a native of the hot countries, and that heated night he bestowed upon his progeny the swanlike grace of his race.

From their mother, Annie, what did they receive? Annie is English, and wan as English weather, so she, too, contributed to the shading of her children. From her the twins get their tendency to cling – which is not surprising. There was little room inside Annie, who was delicately framed, and the twins were forced into the clutches of each other. Annie clung to Kasbah, that heated night; also before that heated night, and forever afterwards as well. Cells multiply, divide, multiply, and eventually grow arms to cling.

The Kesbys had not known they were expecting twins, but the twins knew. The twins knew they were twins before anyone on earth knew it too. These months of shared knowledge meant a great deal to them: they could presume to understand more about one another than anyone else did, because they'd had that private time. They fancied they'd whispered the secrets of Heaven to each other during those months. The womb had been an idyll, a tropical island they'd been washed up on, abundant with food and warmth but secluded, deserted but for them, and they resented the loss of it when the world was hard. They wanted it back, whether the world was hard or not.

Like many twins they were born prematurely, Indigo first and ferocious, Ravel second and bewildered. Indigo was the lion of the pair, he was the one who'd gobbled all the nutrients. This was the baby that Kasbah and Annie had been expecting. The arrival of Ravel, minutes later, was a rude interruption to the merriment in the delivery room. Why had he gone unnoticed, all this time? The lion shields the lamb from probing doctors, from listening ears. Ravel had lain still, his heart beating in time with his brother's.

Indigo they'd settled upon, because it was beautiful. Indigo himself was beautiful. But what to call the half-starved scrag that slithered apologetically into the world in his wake? What else was beautiful (although the scrag itself was not)? The music of Ravel was beautiful.

At home, they screamed all day and night. Kasbah took them out of their separate cots and placed them together in one, but still they howled. Annie hated it, it made her feel shredded, hysterical. Luckily the house was big, a mansion. The house was mansion enough for Annie to escape the sound of the merciless shrieking newborns. From Annie, it might be added, the twins got their money.

'What on earth is the matter with them?' Annie would plead to know.

'They want to go back to where they came from,' is what Kasbah wisely surmised. But where had they come from, these feverish, despotic beings? From her? From him? From space? Kasbah couldn't tell her that.

They stopped crying, as babies will, but not before you think you cannot hear it any more, you'd rather die (or see them die) than survive hearing it any more. Instead, the twins grew silent. Naturally they spoke when spoken to – under begging instruction they would repeat 'doggy' and 'bottle' and 'hello' – but if given the choice they chose to be mute. They tottered about within reach of each other, observing their new realm, swapping significant glances. They began to frown, and their eyes took on an insulted cast. They turned silent and frowning and insulted, and this was unnerving. They seemed unwillingly resigned to their fate now, to this world where grappling hands grasped, more often than not, air. But they also seemed, in their intimacy and their reticence, to be plotting. What do children of two or three or four years plot? They plot to get back what has been taken from them.

8

The twins, thought Annie, were unforgiving.

They went to good schools (Annie's money) and were good at school. They did not make many friends and no one was surprised by this. They were not dislikeable children: they disliked other children. The lion had, by this time, reverted to being a lion cub, and the scrag had caught up to become a cub also, as if Indigo had sacrificed some of his strength in order that his brother should not be left behind. They looked like other children – they looked like the same child. They had nurses and nannies who could not tell them apart. Their parents were far from accurate at distinguishing them – there were too many nurses and nannies. Kasbah and Annie were not so familiar with their offspring that they could be exact. The twins never made use of the resulting confusion, they never deliberately pretended to be each other. Instead, they accepted the confusion: they answered, without comment, if addressed by the wrong name, and more than once they endured, without complaint, punishment for a crime committed by the other. It was as if they didn't mind at all, being mistaken for one another. And it is true that they held each other in high esteem, to the exclusion of all others. They never wanted birthday parties, although they got them, because Annie and Kasbah wished them to be socialised and other parents and children wanted a peek inside the great house. These parties were events of much expense and forced cheerfulness and ended with the twins sullenly, peacefully, locked in their bedrooms, waiting out the day. They were bright children, and knew how bright they were. They partnered each other for school assignments, Indigo the talker-out-loud, the noisy mastermind, Ravel the thinker, leaning against the desk with the pen jammed into his gums. They were quick, but in athletics they raced together, speeding up or slowing down as the other demanded. When one was sick, the other must

9

stay home also, not because they shared physical feeling (this they never did, and scorned suggestion of, as if there was something tacky in the idea) but because the ill one craved the other's company and rallied under this restorative medicine only. Their closeness was accepted because twins are allowed, indeed *expected*, to be close. It was said they would grow apart as they got older, but they never did. Kasbah suggested maybe it was time for another baby; this attempt to somehow loosen the twins' grip was thoroughly knocked on the head by Annie. No, no, no more unexpected scrags. Did she especially resent Ravel, the child who meant Annie would have not one, but none? Not especially. Annie, too, was accepting: she was the type that buys the charming puppy and loathes, yet feels obliged to continue feeding and tending, the rampant hound it becomes. She didn't mind the twins, but they were not what she had expected and would have preferred. Having children was evidently something she and Kasbah failed to do well, and the botch was not to be repeated.

The twins finished school at a blazingly high standard, and promptly went to university. What did they study? They studied life. Medicine? No. Science. They were aware that their fellow students considered them worthy of observation.

And then a strange thing happened: Annie and Kasbah disappeared. Off the face of the earth? No one does quite that. But by the time Indigo read the story about the voraciousness of swine, Kasbah and Annie had been gone for a year and a half, and the twins were twenty-three. Two dark-haired, honey-coloured, identical young men, composites of the world, coloured like the dawn.

A WARNING TO ALL AND SUNDRY

Ravel picked up the book. He flipped through it until he reached the final page, and then he flipped through it backwards. The book told tales of heroism and mercy and unexpected salvations but these didn't interest the twins and scored no points at all and Ravel brushed past them indifferently. He stopped when he found a picture he liked and held up the volume for Indigo to see. Indigo acknowledged the illustration and settled down on his feet.

———

A Coroner's Inquest was held on April 18th, 1821, at Parramatta, New South Wales, investigating the cause of death of one John Buff, who had collapsed and expired some short time beforehand. The Inquest found *that*:

John Buff had spent an afternoon's quiet fishing at Duck-River Bridge, about three miles out from the town of Parramatta. Having filled his bucket to his satisfaction Buff strolled back to Parramatta, which was where he lived, and put a couple of fish in a pot to boil and eat for supper. It had been a fruitful, restful day for him, and while the fish bobbed in their surging water Buff must have yawned and stretched and paced around the room, walking himself awake.

When the time came he accordingly sat down and consumed the fish, and about ten minutes after doing so he found himself growing addled. His tongue swelled until it made him gag. The flatness of the floor beckoned to him and he lay down prone upon it. He begged for water to be brought to him and someone must have brought it, someone who was not suffering the same.

The water having navigated the lumpen tongue, Buff requested to be rolled onto his stomach. Scarcely did the man's nose touch the floorboards than he died, as if the turning had dumped out his soul. The time elapsing between Buff tucking a napkin under his chin and the unfortunate man's departure from the mortal coil was a mere twenty minutes.

Explanation? The TOAD-FISH.

Yes, the toad-fish. Woe betide any man who makes a meal of this disgusting vertebrate. Unblessed by God, the creature is ugly beyond comprehension. Short, fat, coloured unsavoury, with blunt beak of a mouth and ludicrously trimmed fins, who would feel drawn to eat it? Only a fool – or a newcomer to the Colony, blissfully unaware of the poison that cascades through the flesh of this unfavoured beast.

Let this prove a warning to all and sundry.

———

'"It is worthy also of observing",' read Ravel, '"that the deceased expressed no feeling of bodily pain but went off, as it were, in a slumber. Persons that have been bitten by snakes have been affected much in a similar way..."'

He trailed into silence, because he saw he had lost Indigo. His brother was tracing the pattern of the carpet with a fingernail. Ravel let the book tilt over his knees.

'The TOAD-FISH. Didn't you like it?'

Indigo shrugged. 'You should have chosen something different.'

'Why?'

'It was too much like the pig story. No points, for lacking variation.'

Ravel looked crestfallen. The book slipped off his knees and knocked the rim of the plate, bouncing the biscuits into the air. The rats contracted and expanded, agonisingly hesitant.

Indigo unfolded his legs and went to the window. The window reached from his shins to the ceiling and was swathed on each side by scarlet curtain. He put his hands on his hips and sighed, scuffing a foot against the carpet. He was aware of his brother's gaze at his back.

Below Indigo, who stood in the library on the first floor, the front garden stretched the short distance from street to door. There was a fountain in the garden, its bowl brimming with a claggy mulch of leaves, infested with worms and jumping bugs. The grass was long, overgrown, and browned off by the summer heat. Someone had left a child's shirt snagged on a pike of the wrought-iron fence and on this breezeless night it hung still. Still, too, were the rose bushes and the lanky birch. It was possible that even the worms and jumping bugs were still, snug in their decay. There was a moon, but no stars, and the sky was grey rather than dark-blue. Indigo could see the garden clearly thanks to this ghostly sky, and to the streetlight that stood close to the front gate. Across the road there were not houses, but a park. The park was tended; the Kesby residence was not. So, what was brown on one side was echoed on the other in green.

Indigo shifted his stance, to give his twin something to watch.

The concept of the doppelganger – the *double goer* – fascinated humankind well before the Germans gave the name to the notion a long time ago. The real and true definition of a doppelganger is of a shadow-self which follows each one of us, looks exactly like us, and mimics perfectly our movements, our words and inflections, our expressions, everything. It is invisible to all save its owner, and to dogs and cats, which apparently accounts for the scattiness of cats and the startling, unprovoked attacks of dogs. A doppelganger is immune to mirrors: being a reflection, it has none. It is quick, which is why we never see it – it darts agilely behind us when we turn. Why such shyness? A doppelganger does not like to cause its owner shame, which is supposedly what we'd feel if we were to see ourselves. A doppelganger is a benevolent force: it acts as companion, letting us live with ourselves, and occasionally as guardian, halting our step a moment before the pane of glass drops from a sky-scraper, before the wild car comes screeching around the corner. On the other hand, a doppelganger if bored might amuse itself with harmless mischief, such as appearing in places where you are not and thus confusing any friends who might glimpse this false you; sometimes a doppelganger can get very mischievous indeed, putting words into your mouth and deeds into your name, and the result of this is madness.

So, it is best to keep on your doppelganger's good side.

In recent times, the concept of the doppelganger has broadened to encompass the idea that every one of us has a true living double walking around somewhere in the world. The idea is refuted by our knowledge of biology and genes, but still it clings. Why is this? Is it because it comforts us, to imagine there is another who shares our gradual decline? – that the hitherto undiscovered crinkle in the corner of the eye is being noticed by someone else too, someone who will carry the exact same crease (and others that will come) to the grave? Our folds, our tics, our disgusting little sores: all these are suffered the same by another. There's a certain appeal in that.

Or is the walking, talking, breathing doppelganger such a popular fancy because, in truth, we *don't know* what we look like? The faces of other people are much more familiar to us than our own. Is this what intrigues us: the thought that we might not recognise ourselves, were our shoulders ever to bump?

Identical twins know what they look like. Ravel knows that the carved bony wedge of Indigo's elbow is exactly echoed in himself. He knows the shoulder-blades that make moving plateaux in Indigo's back also make plateaux in his own. He knows his own eyelashes; he knows the top of his head and the flesh behind his ears. He knows the nape of his neck, the small of his back, the bridge that divides his nostrils. He knows what he looks like upside-down. There's no singularity in being a twin. The claims of the individual cannot be claimed by the identical twin: what is his to call his own must be bestowed by violence, by the runaway knife that leaves a scar, by the burned-on speckling of the sun. The Kesby twins have largely avoided such violence, and distinguishing marks on them are few.

Ravel, watching Indigo, is caught by the beauty of his brother. He knows the beauty must exist in himself also, but he's never trusted that this is so. He stares in wonder, unconvinced. He has bleak thoughts of himself as a replica – a perfect replica, but nevertheless a replica, which, being imitation, is lesser. And that is far from being what Ravel Kesby wants.

He draws a breath, readying himself. There's no denying he's frightened of his brother, though he knows and loves him so well. He's been frightened of Indigo for a year and a half, but because he's known and loved Indigo so well and so long, Ravel thinks fear is a silly thing to feel. Still, there it is.

———

'I'm thinking of doing something,' said Ravel to his reflection.

'Doing?'

'Something.'

'It's late,' said Indigo, and pressed a hand to the glass. His palm left a print of itself, a doppelganger of dampness. 'It's late to be dancing.'

Ravel cocked his head. He and Indigo never went dancing.

'Let's set fire to the park. We would get a good view from here.'

'. . . I'm thinking of getting a job, maybe.'

Indigo looked over his shoulder. Ravel saw a thousand responses tussle for supremacy. Indigo chose, 'A job? As in, employment for money?'

'Yeah.'

'As in, getting up and going to work every day? Sacrificing all your leisure time?'

'That's what I mean.'

Indigo looked flummoxed. 'I can't believe what I'm hearing,' he said. '*Why* would you want to do that, Ravel?'

'I don't know. I'm bored.'

'You're bored.'

'I'm bored of being here; being nothing.'

'And a job will miraculously transform you into *something*, will it? Good God.'

'That's not what I mean –'

'Well *what*, then?'

'It's just that . . . I never go anywhere, I never do anything . . .'

Indigo stared blankly, his teeth driven into his lip. Ravel grappled for words.

'It's just – what are we going to do, Indi? Are we going to sit here – forever?'

Indigo turned to the window. When he spoke, his voice was crispy around the edges. 'Yes,' he said. 'Until Mum and Dad come back.'

'*Are* they coming back?'

'They'll come back. Everything comes back. The seasons come back. When you cut the grass, it comes back. Comets come back.'

Ravel sighed. It had been summer forever. They never cut the grass. When the comet came it had been too distant to see, so they had to take the newspaper's word for it. 'You get to go out,' he muttered.

'To the *supermarket*. That's not going out. You want to go to the supermarket, you can go. Ha, you'd hate it. The supermarket would kill you.'

'I went to university. That didn't kill me.'

'That was ages ago. It was different, then.'

'I was thinking of going back. But I want a job.'

Indigo was silent for some time. He looked at the ceiling, and at the floor. Ravel curled his toes until they cramped, and prised them straight again. Eventually Indigo said, 'You know, it is a good idea. You could get a job, and I could stay home making dinner for you. Steak. I'll learn to cook steak. Working men need meat. I'll buy cookbooks and oven mittens and steak. Maybe one of those puffy hats as well.'

Ravel smiled. The thought was amusing. He and Indigo ate from tins, most of the time. Indigo rested his head on the windowpane. He laughed, too.

'That's funny, isn't it Rav?'

'Yeah.'

'Yeah, funny. It would give me such a sense of *purpose*, doing that for you. You'd be so smart and clever and employed, and I could be your personal drudge.'

'Well, no –'

'Now Ravel, don't be selfish. That's what I want, to be your drudge. It would give meaning to my existence. I've been practising for the part – I do your washing, I shop for you, I keep the house clean. But if you had a job, oh, that would make it official. I'd be a *professional* drudge then. And you'd be a drone, marching off to work and marching home again. You'd be a real person. God, how I have longed for this day.'

Ravel rubbed sweat from the hollow at his collarbone and waited, while his twin stared peevishly into the garden. 'It wouldn't have to be like that,' he said quietly. 'You could do it too, you could get a job if you wanted –'

'But that's the point, idiot,' Indigo hissed. 'I don't want to. And if I don't want to, how can *you* want to? Have I missed something here? Have you somehow – suddenly – ceased to be my brother, my best friend, Ravel? I've never heard the real Ravel say things like this. The real Ravel doesn't hatch little plans on the side, he doesn't keep secrets, he doesn't talk about leaving me alone while he trots on his merry way. Who are you? Are you some sort of walking, talking, monstrous Ravel?'

'You'd be all right, Indi –'

'Don't tell me what I would be! Go, if you want to, do whatever you like. And if you do go, don't expect things to be the same. Don't think of us being together any more, because we won't be. Everything will change. We won't know each other. After a while, we'll stop caring as much. Then we won't care at all. So go ahead. Go.'

Ravel said nothing. He stared at a biscuit that lay in front of him: it was flat and angular and sprinkled with garish spices.

'I was just thinking about it.'

Indigo said nothing: he waited.

'I wouldn't know what to do, anyway.'

'With a mind like yours, you could do anything.'

'I won't, though.'

'You're young yet.'

Ravel nodded. He scratched at a stain in the carpet as the energy seeped out of him. He had known this was how the conversation would go, could have predicted every word. 'You'd have been all right, though,' he said.

'I know. It was never me I was worried about.'

Ravel bowed his head. Indigo cast off his tension like a coat; he turned and gave his brother a velvety smile.

'It was a nice thought, anyway,' he said.

⁓

Is this the way it is, with twins? Is one always the boss, the other born to kowtow? Like a little slave? Is a bully twin born with his or her own whipping-boy? It certainly seems probable. It is natural that, in all relationships, one party dominates over the other. This is the pecking order, which even chickens have. Nothing is ever equal. Some of us lead, some of us are led. How to tell who is boss, and who is not? I have heard it said that, between lovers and married people, the one who sleeps closest to the door is the boss. This is because the boss is also the protector. Should anything threatening present itself, it is the boss who is expected to defend the pair. This is the price the boss pays, for the privilege of being the boss.

Nonetheless, was Ravel actually as subservient as he

seemed, when he so readily relinquished his intention of getting a job? Not on your nelly.

It's possible Ravel was even brighter than his bright brother. Long ago he'd realised that Indigo was the tyrant of the two. Indigo knew this also, having realised it around the same time. What Indigo didn't know (for tyranny can blind) was that Ravel not only possessed this knowledge, but played upon it ruthlessly. A lifetime of being lesser had allowed Ravel a camouflaged, subversive superiority. He was given no responsibility and so bore none: the luxury was his to be as frivolous and as carefree as he chose. He was heedless to the making of the small daily decisions that concerned him, so his thoughts were unencumbered and roamed as they pleased. Ravel willingly allowed Indigo to lead at all times, with the *exception* of those times when Ravel did not wish to be led.

It was Ravel who dug his heels in, and refused to learn the piano. Indigo learned.

It was Ravel who, aged eight, decided he would no longer go to church. Indigo went until he was twelve.

It was Ravel who suggested Annie and Kasbah could take themselves elsewhere.

And so Ravel, if he'd really wanted to, really would have got himself some job. Indigo thought he had ground the feeble idea to a pulp, but he hadn't. Indigo's tantrums alone would not have dissuaded his twin, who had endured them before. Ravel himself had anaesthetised the idea. He had never worked in his life and was far from sure he ever wanted to. But he wanted to do something.

Ravel was twenty-three. Twenty-three is the age when you realise your life is not only hulking up in front of you, it's also skittering away behind you. An entire third of a reasonably expected lifespan is over. It is a realisation that propels the inactive into action, the morbid into

20

greater morbidity. Ravel wanted to *do* something. He han-
kered for it, as physically as if lacking a vitamin. He
wanted to do *something*. And what did he do? He wandered
in the garden.

The house where the twins lived did not have a yard,
it had a garden. Once it must have had a huge garden,
both front and rear, because the great house demanded it.
Over time, however, and under ownership that lacked
foresight, chunks of the garden had been sold off, giving
the house neighbours so close that their daily activities
could be heard (and monitored, if desired). By the time
the Kesbys bought the house, the enormous structure
loomed over its apron of earth like a raven perched on a
thimble.

The garden had once contained those elements necessary to qualify it as a garden: plants. Technically it still
had them, but the more desirable were no longer very
well, and had become difficult to find. Some plants were
abundant — those of the creeping, mossy or weedy type
thrived. They thrived to the point of suffocation. Now
and then a spindly arm would reach up through the mire,
dangling a fainted lily or sickening camellia, pleading for
attention and rescue, but these were quickly swallowed
again. The garden seemed dangerous, in its ability to do
this. 'It is like,' Ravel decided, '*The Blob*.'

He missed TV.

It was Indigo, not Ravel, who'd decided they no
longer needed to pay the electricity bill. It was Indigo who
presided over matters monetary and he deemed the
expense unjustified. He felt a perverse need to conserve
their income, just in case. The twins had no telephone
line. For over six months they had also had no lighting,
television or refrigeration. The heating and hot water and
the stove ran on gas. The Mercedes in the garage did not.

The Kesby twins were spoilt: all their lives they'd been indulged. Annie and Kasbah *liked* buying them things. They'd bought things for the twins that the twins didn't even *want*. And on their sixteenth birthday, their parents had presented them with credit cards that gained sustenance from Annie's bank account. Annie was a rich woman. She had rich parents six feet under English soil and no grasping siblings. Kasbah was nowhere near as rich as Annie, and his parents and four siblings were alive and prospering, but he did not get along with them. Indigo and Ravel had never even met them.

Thus, no inconvenient familial enquiries into the whereabouts of Annie and Kasbah. What could the twins have said, if there had been? 'We've no idea.'

The credit cards remained linked, by financial umbilical cords, to Annie's bank account. So the twins ate, bought new clothes, went to the Symphony and to midnight sessions at the movies, but did not pay all their bills. The spoilt twins were, in truth, misers. They'd always had a prophet's contempt for the way their parents had splashed the money around. They *liked* the candlelight. It made them feel grandly humble.

The Blob. Trees were planted throughout the old garden, and the new garden was stealthily encroaching upon them, snaking around trunks, sending scouts into the lowest branches. Tendrils of blackberry caught at Ravel's feet as he walked the length of the path. The young thorns were soft and tiny, but sharp enough to ruffle the skin. Like crocodiles, thorns are born with the urge to bite.

Ravel longed, yearned, ached, to *do something*. The gorgeous word *restless* cruised around his head. He whimpered, stamped, kicked a stone from his way. *Restless* is a word that sounds like what it means: it is onomatopoeic.

He stopped, and turned, and looked back the way he

had come. The house sat heavily in the darkness, obscuring the rest of the world. It was a building with no describable shape, for its rooms jutted and folded in on themselves, and there were in total sixteen separate slabs of roof. It was angular, a house made for shadows: shadows were drawn to lurking in corners and under sills. It had been a beautiful house once, a mysterious lady, but Annie and Kasbah had never taken care of it and it was becoming a hag. It had woodworm. Bits of it were starting to teeter and topple off. Its weatherboards needed painting and its roof needed resealing and weeds were sprouting in the troughs of its gutters. Inside, cracks were creeping through the plaster and some of the doors were starting to stick. These things, Ravel knew, would never get the attention they needed.

The highest point of the house was the tower. There was nothing in it, it was not an interesting room. At fifteen and moody Ravel had claimed it as his own, but its view of countless rooves and aerials had wreaked havoc on his angst. He'd abandoned the tower as unRomantic, but his claim on it remained. Now an orange light was glowing from behind its many windows and spreading a sheen against the night, and Ravel lifted a hand and waved to his brother, who might, or might not, have seen.

THE BLOODY TOWER

Richard was a youngest son, and in the 1400s that was a frustrating position to hold. The title 'Duke of Gloucester' had none of the lustre of 'King', which is what they called Richard's brother, Edward IV. But Richard had little chance of becoming King in his own right unless a few people who stood between himself and the mighty chair conveniently disappeared.

There's a painting of Richard in the National Portrait Gallery in London. It depicts a man who seems to bear the worries of the world on his vaguely lopsided shoulders. (Richard was evidently not the freakish crouch-back that Shakespeare makes him out to be. Indeed, contemporary sources make no mention of a deformity and the painting may well have been touched up at a later time, when reputation had got the better of Richard.) He is blue-eyed, his hair is long and curling, and his flesh is so china fragile we can see the veins in the back of his hands. He is a handsome man, but his face and body speak of how anxious he is inside. There are lines around his eyes. He seems on the verge of saying something that he has thought about for a long time. The painting catches him in the act of slipping a ring on – or off – his smallest finger.

Richard fought alongside his brother, the King, during the dynastic Wars of the Roses (Richard and Edward were Yorkists; their rivals to the throne were the Lancastrians). All sources agree that he was a faithful and valiant supporter of his brother, and never shrank from peril.

Edward died on April 9th, 1483, after a short illness. Suddenly the throne gaped vacant. By rights the next to be seated upon it should have been Edward's eldest son, Edward V, who was twelve years old. Richard, who was thirty-one, spotted his only chance.

It's admittable that he had little choice but to do what he did. Had he not seized power the Wydville party, which for years had been angling at the throne and had the child heir very much in its pocket, would have crushed him like a bug. Richard moved to save his skin and it was unfortunate that young Edward happened to be a thorn in that ambitious flesh: Richard grabbed the boy from the clutches of the Wydvilles and popped him into the Tower on May 10th. Having their ace card snatched and a few of their best movers and shakers garrotted seriously corroded the Wydvilles' power base.

There was one untidy remnant left over after the coup, and it had a better claim to the throne than did Richard. Edward's ten-year-old brother Richard, Duke of York, was enticed out of Sanctuary and packed off to join his sibling in the Tower. All that now stood between Richard and the throne was justification, and this was easily trumped up. Richard declared that Edward IV's marriage (to a Wydville) had been illegal, as the monarch had been contracted to marry another at the time of the nuptials; his children, being bastards, could not inherit. No one believed the story but England had a new King: Richard III's reign began on June 26th, 1483.

He was, in fact, a good King. He made quick, firm decisions. He strove for peace and relief for the poor. He beautified his country. A pious, highly cultured and educated man, his court was a haven for scholars and musicians. But being King was a stressful time for Richard. It was stressful because, no matter what worthwhile thing he did, people never took him into their hearts. People insisted on holding a grudge over the fate of those two wretched boys. His friends distanced themselves from him. Plots grew like weeds against him. It is said that Richard's allies stopped their horses and watched him race alone to his death during the battle of Bosworth. It is also said that, once dead, the King was displayed naked in Leicester for two days before being buried in an unmarked grave.

There's a portrait of the boy who would have been King, too. Edward V looks old, for a child. His face is triangular, drawn down with an older man's concerns. He was a careful, thoughtful boy, with intelligence beyond his years. His mouth, though, is a child's mouth – small, soft, pursed. And his eyes look swollen, as if he has been crying.

What did Edward and young Richard think, when they were shepherded into the Tower? They were princes, and used to a cushy life. The Tower had been built in 1078 and was originally used as a fortress to guard the City of London. Four turrets and two lines of fortification protect the vital Keep. The inner line of fortification has twelve towers and it is in one of these that the princes were imprisoned. Their tower became known as the Bloody Tower. But in 1483 the Tower was no rank and

gloomy dungeon. It was actually one of the royal resi-
dences, and had palatial apartments. It held the Mint and
many offices, and it had a zoo that was open to the public.
The Tower would not have been a place of terror in the
memory of the two boys. The rooms they occupied were
beautiful. But Edward V was a clever child, and he sus-
pected he was unlikely to see beyond the stone walls
again. He lived in a time of violence and there was many
a precedent for the disposal of a rival to the throne. When
his little brother joined him in captivity he must have
guessed his time was nearly up. The murders are thought
to have taken place on September 3rd, by which date
Edward had been imprisoned for just over three months,
and Richard for just over two.

What did they talk about, in all that time? Edward
doubtlessly tried to shield his brother, a playful and viva-
cious boy, from the truth that was coming for them. He
probably tried to talk of things that made Richard happy
and made him laugh. Maybe they plotted daring escapes.
They might have recalled the fun things they had done.
They no doubt talked about their parents.

Were they ever cold? Did they ever cry? When fate
unlocked their door on the night of September 3rd, were
they given any time, to cry?

That the princes died in the Tower, there is little
doubt. Remains of two small skeletons were found in a
chest beneath a stairwell of the Tower in 1674, and tests
show they are almost certainly the bones of the princes.
Now those bones lie in the more sacred, but no less cold
and vault-like, surrounds of Westminster Abbey. This is a
certainty, but it is one of few. If you read on this subject,
you will come across the words 'probable' and 'likely' and
'circumstantial' with dreary frequency. No one who was
directly involved in the story bothered (or was able) (or

lived long enough) to write the facts down. So, it's *highly likely* that Richard snuffed the princes, but the evidence is *circumstantial*. Henry VII, to whom the living princes would have been a threat, has been a suspect, but the rumour against him doesn't hold. The year 1483 is *thought to be* the year the brothers died, but only because no one saw them after that date. How they died is *unknown*. It's *possible* they were smothered, or poisoned.

In the end, the things we imagine are the things that surely come closest to the truth. The princes must have been confused and frightened. They were just children. And King Richard, who wanted so much to be a good man, must have felt a snag of guilt.

But, in the end, who did what when doesn't really matter. That it was done at all is the point of the tale.

⎯⎯•⎯⎯

Indigo watched his brother, who was sleeping. The night was almost over. The heat had flattened Ravel: he lay deep in the padding of the couch, his chest hardly lifting, his limbs cast out as if he'd finished with them. When he woke he'd find that his sweat had sealed him to the leather of the Chesterfield, and getting to his feet would sting.

Conversations swirled around in Indigo's head. Indigo Kesby's mind was as fidgety as a sparrow.

'Look at you two,' said Annie. 'You're grown up now.'

Ravel lifted his head. He was eating cereal, the bowl up close to his chin. He wore pyjamas and a dressing-gown, although it was past midday on a Sunday. He was, at that time, in love, though Indigo couldn't bring himself to apply that particular potent, embracing, excluding word to a relationship that had lasted scarcely three months. Ravel had besotted himself with thoughtless haste, in Indigo's opinion, and with undignified abandon. Ravel had tried to enthuse his brother to his happiness and Indigo had been offended by the attempt. Indigo thought of the girl as one might think of a repulsive insect that has taken up residence on one's ceiling: irately, compulsively. He wanted a glimpse of her. He didn't want an introduction, he didn't want to touch her or talk to her: he wanted her measure. One day he shadowed Ravel to her house and as she opened the door his mind snapped down on her image like a shutter, never to be forgotten, nemesis. A small thing to cause him disruption. Driven by curiosity but against his better instincts he once had to ask, 'What have you told her about me?'

Ravel, stalling, replied, 'Huh?'

'What have you told her about me?'

'Nothing.'

'Nothing?'

'She doesn't ask.'

'*Nothing?*'

'We don't talk about things like that.'

'Things?'

'I've told her I've got a brother.'

'A brother?'

Ravel glanced up, amused. 'Why are you repeating everything I say?' he asked.

Indigo blinked several times, wounded by the extent of his exclusion. His words stuttered through his shock. 'I'm your *twin*, Ravel,' he said. 'I'm not your *brother*.' This was enough to make the point, but he tacked on viperishly, 'Up until recently I have been the most important person in your life.'

Ravel did not flinch. 'All right,' he said. 'I'll tell her.'

He told her, and reported back, 'She wants to meet you.'

It was Indigo's turn to glance up, and he refrained from doing so.

'I told her about you, and now she wants to meet you.'

29

'I,' sniffed Indigo, 'don't care for it.'

Ravel was unruffled. He would not be dissuaded from his affection, his merry tales would not be silenced, his smile would not be smashed. He couldn't be convinced that his romance was tedious. Twenty-one years old and in love for the very first time, his joy eluded all attempts to muffle it. And then the girl broke the thing apart.

She cited a litany of hollow reasons for doing so: she was busy with her studies, she hadn't the time to put in a commitment, he didn't like dancing, he didn't get on with her friends – he deserved someone better than she. Ravel, though a novice, understood what these reasons, condensed and purified, meant: they meant, *I do not love you.*

Is there ever a more grievous injury inflicted than that which the unwanted lover receives? It is a cleaving knowledge, that one is unlovable to the one who is adored. Heartbroken, Ravel plummeted into the hunting-ground of depression as if this was what he'd sought all along: not to be cherished, but to be damned. He turned his heart against himself: unloved, he was unlovable. He hated himself, and hatred made him rancorous. The mundane made him want to scream. And his mother, it suddenly seemed, was the Queen of the Mundane. Ravel looked at her with murderous eyes.

'You make me lose my appetite,' he said, and dumped his breakfast on the kitchen table. Milk and sodden flakes sloshed over the rim of the bowl. His mother and father cringed away from him. Indigo, who was standing idle waiting for the kettle to boil, felt his brother's frustration cloud over him, a doppelganger of discontent.

'It was only an observation,' said Kasbah.

'Grown up now,' chanted Ravel. 'Of course we're grown up now. What did she expect? We'd be stunted? Children forever? Why does she say such stupid, pointless things?'

Annie, whose grasp on serenity was always tentative, fluttered her hands to her face. Ravel watched her, disgusted. 'Go on,' he jeered. 'Cry.'

'Be nice to your mother,' said Kasbah. He put an arm around his wife and she buried her face in his shoulder.

'I don't see why I should. She is not nice to me. I hate the way she bawls. She's an actress, she turns them on like a tap. I hate her. I hate everything about her.'

Indigo stared at his brother. He knew what was coming, he knew the words Ravel would go on to say. Many times the twins had spoken them to each other.

'She never calls me by my name,' Ravel told his father. 'Have you noticed? She never says Indigo, she never says Ravel. Do you know why? She's afraid she'll get it wrong. She can't tell which of us is which.'

'That's not true.' Kasbah hugged his wife's yellow head.

'No? Who am I? Mother, who am I?'

Annie gave a strident sob. Ravel clenched his fists.

'Am I Indigo?' he asked. 'Am I Ravel? Are the names we call ourselves the names you christened us with? Or did we have to settle the matter between ourselves? Am I Indigo? Does it matter? I don't suppose it does. We're the same, a single entity. We're *the twins*, aren't we? That's how you introduce us to your friends. Not *our twins* or *my twins*. Just *the* twins. On the back of photos we're *twins*. Alone, we're *twin*. We hate you for that, Mother. We hate you for not knowing the difference. It makes me want to kill you.'

'Ravel, please,' whispered Kasbah, as Annie clawed at his throat. Ravel looked away, revolted.

⟞⟝

Does all this sound criminally disrespectful? There's a Commandment, isn't there, about respecting one's mother and father? Pagan Ravel.

31

But what is one to do, when one's parents aren't deserving of respect? It's difficult, isn't it, to respect the neglectful, the untrustworthy, the dictatorial and the abusive, or the failure whose aspirations would drive a child into the ground?

Annie and Kasbah could be accused of none of these greater crimes. Their crimes were subtle, evident only to the victims. And, oddly enough, the twins disagreed on which crime was the most offensive, the most in need of punishment.

As a child, it had not unduly bothered Ravel that his parents could not differentiate him from his twin. It was probable that all identical twins lived amidst such blatant befuddlement. And it was flattering, sometimes, to be mistaken for Indigo, who was brave and strong and generous and an intrinsically better person than Ravel knew himself to be. Older, Ravel grew wiser, but his parents did not. Their incompetence in the matter of which twin was which seemed less like normality, more like negligence.

Indigo took umbrage at something far less concrete.

When Annie and Kasbah were out in public, they *looked*. He was young when he first became aware of it, and he watched it become a habit. Annie and Kasbah looked at other people's children. What was in their eyes, when they were looking, was envy. The discovery horrified Indigo, then enraged him. *Envy!* The insult of that green emotion was indescribable. Ravel, told of it, had watched for it, had failed to find it, but believed Indigo that it was there.

Though their opinions differed on the degree of vileness of each misdeed, the twins very much agreed on what, in the best of all worlds, would be the ideal solution to the situation.

———

'We've been thinking,' said a timid Kasbah. Ravel didn't bother to look at him. 'We've been thinking, perhaps the two of you would like to go away, somewhere?'

'You're sending us away?'

'Only on a holiday. It might be nice for you.'

'Nice for us? To be sent away?'

Kasbah steeled his courage. His children unnerved him: he'd never intended they should be the way they were. 'You've finished your schooling,' he said. 'Now's the time to see the world. It would be fun for you. You wouldn't have to go to the same places. One could go to Europe, we thought, and the other could go to –'

'Hell?' Ravel suggested. Kasbah clicked shut his jaw. Ravel smiled unhappily, and gazed around the room. Indigo watched – felt – him wrestle with his fury, his broken heart. The kettle was billowing out steam that fogged the kitchen window and made Indigo feel raw.

'You've wanted us to go away since the day we were born,' Ravel said finally.

'Don't be ridiculous –'

'You've never known what to do about us. We're not what you expected, are we? We're not like you, or her. That's why you never say *my twins*, isn't it, Mother? Because we're not yours. You'd rather we weren't yours. We're cuckoos, aren't we? Cuckoos in your wooden nest. Where's your real child? There must have been only one – two is clumsy, after all. Two means that there's nothing for you. Maybe your real child is playing tennis. Maybe it's shopping. Maybe it's trying on clothes. Maybe it's gone out for lunch. Maybe it's laughing. Maybe it's dead.'

Annie put her hands to her ears. She sucked in air and sobbed. Kasbah clutched her to his chest.

'We're not toys,' Ravel said. 'We're not decoration.

33

We're not trivial. We don't care about the things you care about. We don't cry.'

'That's enough now, stop.'

'And so you want to send us away. . .'

Ravel appeared to turn the proposition over in his mind. He looked at his father, and at the back of his mother's head.

'I'm sorry,' he said, 'but we don't want to go. We like it here. Things would be better if *you* went. Yes, we'd like it much better if the pair of *you* went away. We can live without you, you know. We do it already.'

———

Indigo reached out and took his brother's hand. It had been the strangest morning. The kitchen had filled with steam until they could scarcely see through the mist. Indigo had sought for his twin, to see the expression on his face. For the first time it occurred to him that, in the womb, they must not have been able to see each other. It would have been dark in there. Each must have known of the other's existence through touch alone. The knowledge, then, was enough: they didn't need to see, to know.

Ravel was sweating. His hand left a curled wet image of itself on the leather. Indigo searched for something cool to wipe over him. The room was filled with books and the sunrise, and that was burning hot.

That morning, Indigo had burned inside, to hear the words so long whispered finally spoken aloud.

———

Indigo stepped through the clouds. He could not believe he'd heard the things that had been said. He admired his brother, at that moment, more than he could say.

'Ravel,' he said. He spoke gently, and calmly. He thought his twin might be in shock, or hysterical. Ravel lifted his gaze from where it had fallen to the table-top.

'It's Indigo, Ravel.'

'Indigo,' said Ravel, 'why don't you turn off that fucking kettle?'

'Come outside, Ravel, with me.'

Indigo led his brother outside, into the wintry afternoon. He propped his twin against a garden wall. He smoothed the hair from Ravel's face and wiped away the milk between his fingers. They could hear voices coming from the house. The twins were being discussed.

'Everything I said was true.'

'Yeah.'

'You know it too.'

'Of course, Ravel.'

'I wish they *would* go.'

'And that's true, too?'

Ravel faltered, and gave a brittle laugh. He looked at the hand that Indigo held, carefully cleaned, lying like a specimen flat out on Indigo's palm. 'They don't love us,' Indigo reminded him.

'No, not very much.'

'Not at all. And they're our parents.'

'It makes me sad.'

'They want to separate us.'

'Yeah.'

'They're as bad as that girl you knew.'

Ravel's mouth curled sourly. 'Yes,' he said.

'It should make you angry.'

'It does,' Ravel confirmed. 'It does make me angry.'

Indigo nodded. 'Stay here,' he said. 'Stay out here and don't come inside until I call you.'

By the time Indigo called him, several hours later, Ravel had become well acquainted with the rear garden. It would never look the same as it had that day. It started its self-suffocation, its slow, smothering overgrowth, that very afternoon.

⌒

In times of drought or over-population or simple scarcity, the rabbit employs a talent that enables it and its kin to cope with the hardship of the situation. A female rabbit, full of young at that time, has the ability to *absorb* her babies, effectively reducing them to nothing. When times are once again bountiful and additional rabbits can be accommodated by the environment, the female rabbit allows those postponed babies to develop again, and bears them into a world that is fit for another generation.

Where do those baby rabbits go, when they are absorbed? How can something exist, yet not? How can it be alive, and have no form? How does a heartbeat wait?

To Ravel it seemed that his parents completely disappeared, but continued to exist in some far-off, unspecified place that he needn't visit or think about. This arrangement delighted him. It is a divine sensation, when the unwanted get what they want, and what Ravel wanted was a victory to soothe his horrible defeat. He paraded through his usurped castle, chortling, bubbling with satisfaction. He made a proud point of never asking what had become of the two quaking figures he'd last seen enveloped in steam. He left Indigo to take care of everything, because Indigo was practical, and practised.

With time, however, Ravel grew jittery. Public opinion did not turn against him, as it had with Richard, for there was no public of any consequence in the life of the twins. Ravel grew jittery of Indigo, the only one who mattered. Indigo assured him his vanished parents were safe, but where exactly is it that the safely vanished vanish to? Indigo never was specific, and Ravel asked less and less. Indigo began to quietly advise, and Ravel felt an

36

uneasy compulsion to obey. Ravel shouldn't go about alone . . . Ravel probably should not leave the premises. Ravel should confine his wanderings to the rear garden. Ravel should not stand at any window. Whenever possible, it was best that Ravel stayed deep within the house. Indigo's would be the face that was seen by the world. Indigo would deal with it.

'Why?' Ravel queried. 'What does it matter? No one can tell us apart.'

'Some people can,' his brother assured him. 'For some people, we're as different as peas in a pod.'

But, for most people, there ceased to exist twins. In place of two there was one, and the boy who wandered in the garden was the same boy who stood, hands on hips, staring imperiously from the library window.

———

Indigo sat back and watched his brother sleeping. Ravel, the accident, the unexpected. Ravel's existence gave Indigo something most people do not have: another life. He could behave as he chose, confident that his other, concurrent life (titled *Ravel*) would smooth any edges he ruffled. Through Ravel, Indigo was kind and humorous and giving and naive. Indigo loved the Ravel side of himself much more than he loved the Indigo side.

Indigo's was a greedily possessive love, and he would have argued that this is what love must be. He did not say *the* brother, he said *my* brother. He would say he owned Ravel, because he loved him. He loved him *because* he owned him, as one loves what one owns. The fact that he owned Ravel *ensured* that Indigo loved him.

And now Ravel was restless. Indigo could smell the sensation on his skin, feel it turning like a grub in his brother's brain. It was something that lived, but had no form.

37

Ravel did not want to be a twin any more. Ravel wanted separation.

Indigo's love for his twin was a clashing, grinding, violent thing – a love that soared so close to the pinnacle of possibility that it required only the slightest nudge to dislodge it. As love falls, it sometimes transforms itself into the one thing that will have a cushioned landing: a serpent of foul-mouthed hatred. Like a dog deranged in a brawl, Indigo turned upon the one that was his ally.

'My hungry piglet,' he murmured sweetly. 'My poisonous little toad-fish. How could you?'

He raised a hand and slapped his brother hard across the face, and as Ravel recoiled into consciousness Indigo asked blandly, 'What? You were having a dream.'

IT SHOULD BE NEEDLESS TO ADD

With Annie and Kasbah freshly gone, the twins were free to rifle like rats through the house. They had always done so anyway: their parents kept nothing that the twins did not know about. There was new exhilaration, however, in the unspoken understanding that what they found was now theirs to keep. What they found was: rats. The huge house abounded with rats that heard the silence and crept from the walls as a multitude. Born shy, they quickly grew bold. The firm grey bodies would skitter up the stairs, dodging each other and the twin that they raced. They would sidle across an occupied room and pause halfway, lifting whisk-ered snouts to gauge the mood. To open a cupboard was to see a thin black tail whipped out of view. The squeals that accompanied their incessant squabbling found exit through the cracks in the walls. Ravel tolerated their pres-ence but would not let them near him; Indigo could recog-nise individuals, and fed them scraps from his hand.

The other thing the twins found was the library. Nat-urally they'd known of the library since their childhood, and as children they had scribbled upon many a book shelved in it. It was their father's library and the scholarly twins had regarded it as another child might regard its parents' music collection: fascinating for the first ten years, antiquated and embarrassing for the following ten, and then as something to rediscover with a broader, more lenient disposition. These relics are an insight into the mind of another, but more interesting than that is the insight they provide into one's own mind. They are memory capsules. The old tunes are given place, and past.

In the library the twins found many of the books they'd scribbled on. Ravel turned the volumes round and around, trying to decipher what he'd drawn. Time and again they found their names practised in quaking hands, the pencil pushed hard against the soft page, INDIGO in green, RAVEL in red. The letters stood perkily to attention but facing the wrong direction, like troops unable to perfect the drill. They found on the shelves the oddest volumes, testimony to their father's quirky taste, a taste his children had inherited, that finds pleasure in oddity. They found books on myth, on medicine, on history, on psychology, demonology, on anatomy, on sex. They found books on twinship. They found books whose words were shielded by tissue, words printed on paper you could eat. They found postcards and photographs slipped between the pages. They found the book they read so often to each other.

The book has magical qualities. Ravel Kesby might flick through it, back and forth, a thousand times, and still find a story he has not encountered before. The book has pictures and a range of different typefaces. In it exists a tale for every occasion. Ravel is interested only in the most eccentric of them, the ones that make the world an understandable, forgivable place.

—◆—

Four men were convicts: John Cox, John Phillips, John Place, and William Knight. They sailed out on the ship *Glatton* and were put to work at Castle-Hill. Aboard ship, and labouring amongst the rock-breakers, they heard a rumour that they listened to with interest: China, and liberty, lay directly across the mountains.

They escaped with apparent ease. Each left armed with his week's rations. Within five days all the food was gone.

They travelled for seventeen days, the pale sun always over their right shoulder. Of the seventeen days, twelve were stumbled through on stomachs rattling with the few bitter wild-currants they managed to scrounge. The mountains were endless and unconquerable in this state of near-starvation, and the four men resolved to turn back.

This decision made, John Phillips felt bolstered enough to gather berries for the trip. The lone survivor of the attempt would later testify that they heard Phillips call for help several times but could render him no assistance. It is assumed he dropped over the edge of a cliff and eventually died.

Three days later, the remaining escapees were within five miles of Richmond-Hill and release from the torturous journey. Perhaps they did not know salvation was so close at hand: why else would William Knight lie down and refuse to travel any further? It is assumed he eventually died.

Place and Cox shambled on. They reached a river, and in the crossing the current wrenched them apart. Place hauled himself to the far bank and looked around to see Cox, on the opposite bank, stark-faced and prone with exhaustion. The river had stripped him of everything except his shirt and shoes. Place left him, as he'd left them

41

all, and, the night being extremely cold, it is assumed Cox died.

John Place tottered between realities. Frail with hunger and fraught with hopelessness, he too lay down to die. The following day he was found by natives hunting for kangaroo. Place was dragged mindless, but alive, to the nearest hut.

⌁

'"The above awful admonition",' read Ravel, '"will deter all others who do now or shall in future, entertain any idea of regaining their liberty by a similar act". I don't *think* so.'

He was about to close the book when the final line caught his eye and sent him tumbling with laughter.

IT SHOULD BE NEEDLESS TO ADD, read the smug broadside, THAT CHINA DOES NOT LAY BEYOND THE MOUNTAINS.

⌁

Indigo was in the kitchen. He'd been to the supermarket and returned. He had unpacked the groceries and given each item its place on the table and when Ravel walked into the room he was staring without satisfaction at this assemblage of the things he'd bought. The kitchen was built against an outer wall, so servants and delivery men might access it without traipsing through the house and disturbing the occupants. Ravel had been reading in the coolness of the dining-room, deep in the dark heart of the house, and entering the kitchen blinded him. He felt for the table-top and sat down, clearing a space for the book. A packet of frozen chips dropped heavy to the floor. Rats, spying through knotholes, restrained their reflexes.

'Listen, Indi,' he said. He waited a minute until his dazzled vision became clear. '*Fatal Attempt to Escape to China.* Sydney, June 26th, 1803.'

He read aloud the tale of the ill-fated escape while

42

Indigo stood and watched him, saying nothing, and the rats deliberated on crossing the floor to investigate the frozen chips. Ravel concluded his reading with a flourish. He lifted his voice and announced sternly that China, despite all rumours, did not lie, and had never lain, beyond the mountains.

'Hmm,' said Indigo.

'Ten points?'

'Whatever.'

Ravel stroked the page with the back of his hand. 'Didn't you like it?'

'I suppose. No.'

'Why not?'

'It didn't have . . . details.'

'Like what?'

'Like, if they died, and there's no proof they did, why didn't the survivors eat them?'

Ravel chuckled, but Indigo didn't smile. He looked hot and tired.

'It was good, though – that one man escaped. Free.'

'I doubt he escaped. The story wouldn't be recorded if he'd escaped. Someone caught him, and wrote that story down. The man himself probably got sent straight back to cracking rocks. He deserved worse.'

'Oh, why?'

'Because,' said Indigo, 'he abandoned. He left the ones who'd gone through everything with him, and he didn't care what happened to them.'

'He had to survive,' Ravel replied. 'He did what he did to keep himself alive.'

'He was selfish,' Indigo snapped. 'I hate that in a person. He should have died, for being such a bastard. No points.'

Ravel shut the book on his fingers and surveyed the

table. Indigo had a core group of necessities that he bought every week. Toffee-apples, sugary cereal, muffins pocked with sultanas. These things did not need freezing or refrigeration. They were packaged in plastic or aluminium or cardboard. Muesli with chocolate . . . cola cordial . . . cream crammed inside an aerosol tin. Miniature bottles of vodka, and lime juice inside a plastic lime decorated with a plastic leaf. The frozen chips were a novelty and Indigo scooped them off the floor. They had to be eaten immediately.

'You're getting difficult to please, Indi.'

'No, I am not.'

'I can't please you any more.'

'No,' said Indigo, as the chips avalanched onto a tray. 'You cannot.'

Ravel propped his chin in his palm. His twin lit the stove and slid the tray into the cavern. He closed the oven door and dashed droplets from his hands.

'Someone asked about you, down at the shops,' he said.

'Me? Who?'

'Mrs Giotto. She called me Ravel. You must have left an impression: she was so excited at meeting you that I felt obliged to point out her error. No, I said, I'm Indigo. It's a common mistake.'

'Mrs Giotto? I don't know any Mrs Giottos.'

'Yes you do.' Indigo was walking to the pantry and back, positioning goods on shelves. 'She had that funny speech thing. She used to clean the house.'

'Mrs Giotto?'

'When we were kids. Sometimes she cooked. She cooked rissoles. Remember – she always had cat hair on her clothes. You asked her if we were eating cat hamburgers. God, you were so impertinent when you were a kid.'

'What colour hair did she have?'

44

'Black.'

'Was she short?'

Indigo said, 'Yeah,' from inside the pantry.

'Thin?'

'She's not thin any more. She's fat, and her hair is grey. She's still short, though. Shorter, I think.'

Ravel pouted, and shook his head. 'I don't remember her at all,' he said.

'Well, she remembered you. She said, Ow is little Wavel?'

'What did you say?'

'I said, Wavel is fine.'

Ravel nodded. It was interesting, and pleasing, to be remembered by someone he'd forgotten. Indigo heaped powdered milk into a jug and carried the jug to the sink He let the water run until it was cold, then tilted the jug under the tap. The powder surged, dispersed, turned the water an impure white.

'She said, I aven't seen your pawents lately. Ow are they? Are they keeping well? And I said, Oh, they've gone away. On oliday? Yep, on holiday.'

Ravel eyed his brother, heard the chips brightly spit.

'Are they gone for a lengthy time, Inigo? Well, Mrs Giotto, we're not sure. Certainly they've *been* gone a lengthy time. They had to go, you see. Wavel wanted them to go.'

'You said *that*?'

Indigo stirred the milk with a wooden spoon. He tapped the spoon against the rim of the jug until the globules of powder broke from it and swirled away. 'It just slipped out,' he said.

'Jesus, Indigo —'

'It's true, though. It's what you said you wanted them to do.'

'Yes, but I didn't mean – I didn't mean it like that. You shouldn't have said –'

'*I'm* not the one who said anything, Wavel.'

Ravel fell silent. It filled him with terrible unease, to talk of his vanished parents. He didn't want Indigo to talk about it either. Indigo waited, and swung away. He rinsed two glasses and popped the lid from a tin of granuled peppermint flavouring. He put a tablespoon of flavouring in each glass and poured the milk on top of it. The milk changed colour to an unsavoury livid green. He pushed a glass across the table to his brother and considered the depths of his own drink.

'You're right,' he said. 'I shouldn't have said it.'

'No, you shouldn't.'

'She was such a gossip,' he mused. 'Remember, she used to come to work with stories about everyone. He did this, she said that. Isn't it shocking how, I do think they should have, I overheard, I saw on the stweet . . . I've only just remembered what a mouth she had. She was a blathering old bitch, really. You better stay low for a while. If she sees you, she'll have a thousand questions. Have they gone to Italy? Do they send postcards? Do they need a cleaning lady? You better be careful.'

'I *am* careful. I'm always careful. You're always telling me to be careful, and I *am* –'

'It's *easy* for you to be careful. I've *made* it easy for you to be careful. You don't have to see anyone, you don't have to think on your feet. It's a hundred degrees out there. I was hot, I have a headache, I had spaghetti tins taking chunks out of my shins. I have to cope with people and questions whether I want to or not. I cope, so you won't have to. You can't blame me if I make an occasional faux pas.'

Ravel couldn't think of a reply. He stared at his

brother until his brother looked down and muttered, 'Drink your milk.'

The milk left green traces around Ravel's mouth. While they ate the chips Indigo spoke of the checkout boy at the supermarket who had promised ominously that the heat-wave would continue. It said so on the TV. Television was for small minds. Small minds believed the TV. Still, you couldn't deny that it was hot. This was weather to be respected. Ravel nodded several times. He toiled to eat his lunch. Eventually Indigo asked him, 'Are you all right?'

'I just wish you hadn't said –'

'No, I don't mean that. I mean, do you feel all right?'

'All right?'

'You don't look well. You look pale. Like you're sick.'

Ravel paused. 'I'm hot,' he said.

'Everyone's hot. Have you got a temperature?'

'I don't know. I don't think so.'

'Just the weather.'

'I feel a bit queasy. I might have a virus.'

'It's the weather. Have a cool bath.'

Ravel sighed. He ate a few chips. Then he pushed his plate away. 'I can't eat these,' he said. 'My appetite is gone.'

'It doesn't matter.'

Ravel slumped in his seat, disgruntled. He watched his twin, who kept his head bowed. Indigo was fastidious, and he cleaned his fingers carefully after handling each parched and rigid chip. He had always been that way, fussy: when he was a boy he used to tidy Ravel's room, making the bed up, tossing out the treasures. Ravel would be furious, and Indigo would be on his knees rummaging through the rubbish bins. And it would all happen again, another day: Indigo couldn't help himself. The recollection made Ravel feel bleakly cruel.

'I'm sorry, Indi,' he said.

Indigo lifted his eyes and smiled. 'What for?'

'I don't know ... for everything. For everything and always.'

Indigo laughed lightly. 'You always were prone to pity. It will be the death of you, Ravel. You're sick already, see? Leave the chips, if you don't want them. The rats will finish off for you.'

Ravel nodded agreement, to this unpleasant thought.

THE ESSENCE OF TREES

Ravel bounced a tennis ball against the garden wall. It was an old ball, and had been warping in the weather for some time, but under the influence of his grip and throw it flew fast and straight, colliding against the stone and returning faithfully to him, finding his hand as if it had eyes of its own.

He stood in the garden, pointlessly hurling the ball. The sun needled down on him, daring him back into the shade of the house. Ravel was stubborn in his refusal and each drop of sweat that slipped down his shoulders and sogged into his t-shirt was a victory for him, not for the heat of the day.

The ball made a clean and pleasant *thunk* as it slammed against the wall. The noise counted off the moments, though Ravel had long lost his place in the counting. The rhythm was soothing enough. The ball left shreds of itself in the creases of his palm, minute scraps of its fuzzy hide, specks of dirt that had gathered to it over time. It made his flesh feel gristly.

He had been thinking through the night. Ravel was

a calm, professional thinker. He'd thought calmly about Mrs Giotto, and what Mrs Giotto might mean. He was worried by her, by her sudden presence in his present, more so by her absolute absence in his past. The name meant nothing to him. Indigo had remembered her clearly, had recognised her immediately, but to Ravel she was simply fiction. He was losing – had lost – a piece of his past.

We, as humans, forget things. On our deathbeds we are forced to review our lives as a series of events – events that may or may not connect in some gratifying, fated way, but events, blocks of history. It matters not what these events are, or their degree of importance: they are remembered, and they therefore become our life. The things we do not remember are the millions and millions of small details that surrounded these events, led up to them, trailed away from them: that is, we fail to remember the threads that link the events. Most of our day-to-day thoughts, activities, and words, are cleanly forgotten. We forget conversations, quips, passing comments. We forget small journeys. We forget the incidents that seem, to us, unremarkable. And this is regrettable.

Look at a tree. A tree appears to be nothing but a solid thing. The hallmark, the very essence of a tree, lies in its solidity. Yet, inside the tree, countless litres of water are being powerfully pumped, up and up, up the great trunk, along the network of branches, out to each and every leaf, out to the most insignificant twig. A tree is a gurgling, driving, fluid thing. The heart of a tree lies in liquid. To see only the solidity of the tree is to overlook the truth of the tree. So it is with the events that make us who we are. On our deathbeds we must feel oddly one-dimensional. We see the solidity of ourselves: the events. Yet who we are is refined by what we say, think, and feel:

50

the liquid of our lives. And that is what we lose.

But Ravel, like his brother Indigo, had always had the advantage of a second life. A life lived concurrently but a second life nonetheless. Two minds, to remember. Two memories focused on one lifetime. He should forget less, he reasoned, than singular people. But he *was* forgetting, drifting, in his restlessness, from this place where he was anchored. Wanting a life, he was losing the one he had. He was living in a box, and the box was getting smaller.

The ball went *thunk, thunk*. The garden wall was made of stone, like the wall of a fortress. A strong hard wall to protect the vulnerable heart, the house, which was only made of wood, and prey to all that ails and damages wood.

Once, Indigo had found a story in a newspaper and the twins agreed it was a fifty-pointer. It was the story of a girl who lived in her bedroom for ten years. The neighbours remembered her as a bright, bossy child who had one day ceased to be seen. She was found, ten years later, when ambulance officers were called to the family home. The girl had died of pneumonia and been laid out on the kitchen table. The ambulance men noted that her body was hunched and deformed and that her fingernails were incredibly long but her toenails were stubby and short. This was because, at some point, the girl had stopped walking, and begun to crawl. The bedroom she'd lived in for a decade was empty of furniture and in disrepair: its walls, its floor and ceiling were scrawled upon and punched in. The most amazing revelation was that the girl had *chosen* to live her life that way. Her family hadn't locked her up. Indeed, they adored her, and were shattered by her death. She'd let herself be locked up of her own free will. She'd locked herself up.

'Why would anyone do it?' Ravel had asked, and Indigo had answered, 'Things just go that way sometimes.'

And they do. Ravel often thought of that girl. He wished he could have talked to her, asked her what she remembered. He wanted to map the path she'd taken to her bedroom, to understand the liquid of her life. He wanted to ask her about the box she lived in and how she found satisfaction in passing her life that way. Sometimes he wanted to grab her and shake her, and sometimes he thought of her as a friend. Once he experimented stumping around the house on his hands and knees but after an hour it hurt his wrists and skinned his feet and Indigo hauled him to a standstill.

The ball was flying harder and faster, and the easy *thunk* had risen in pitch to become a strung-out *ping*. The ball stung, when it slapped back into his palm. It whistled as it barrelled through the air. Standing in the garden, burning in the sunshine and breathing the gusting air, Ravel felt cloaked by something heavy and dark and cool.

The ball hit a new spot on the wall, a fraction left of where it was supposed to go. It ricocheted like a bullet and vanished in a blink. Ravel stood stunned. He felt robbed, dumped, assaulted. It took a minute for him to collect himself. The spell was broken, but he did not want it to be. He had liked the place where he had been, the place of *thunk* and *ping*. He tugged at the t-shirt until it peeled away from his skin, and went in search of the ball.

He rummaged through the silvery grass, down on his hands and knees. The sweep of his hands drove insects into the air. The tiny creatures went for his eyes, his mouth, his nose: their inclination to do so struck him as perverse. The grass was dry and caught at his fingers and when a blade cut into him he sat back, nursing the small wound sulkily, and stared around. In the wilted brown jungle of the rear garden there were a thousand places a tennis ball could hide. Looking, he saw the light.

It glowed from the underground and Ravel padded through the grass to reach it. Close to the side of the house the vegetation was denied the steaming summer showers by the reach of the eaves high above. The plants that had grown flush against the house were long dead; the weeds that took their place had become sparse, brittle, and grey. Ravel flattened himself to the earth and peered through the stalks.

The house concealed a maze of servants' rooms. Space for them had been gouged from the ground and the house had been built above them. None who saw the house could have guessed the existence of these rooms, and that was how it was meant to be. The builder had allowed the servants light, but not too much: a row of narrowest windows ringed the house, battling to keep their sills above the earth. A servant could not see out these windows without the additional height of a chair beneath the feet, and then the view would consist of fallen leaves, tree roots, birds ploughing worms, and everything else that the very lowest of the low might see. Anyone looking in through the windows from the outside, as was Ravel, was offered a view of the rooms from the lofty position of a god.

Indigo had left a candle burning and Ravel, scarcely believing his eyes, pushed himself to his feet.

———

RAT: common name for any large member of the rodent family Muridae. Rats are dull in colour; their hair is coarse and lies close to the body. The tail is long and of a scaled appearance; the ears are large in comparison to the animal's overall size. Rats have sharp and sturdy teeth which are rooted deep in their skulls and are continuously growing: a rat must gnaw to keep these teeth manageable and at bay. Rats can chew with little difficulty through wood, and lead. They are nocturnal animals by nature, but they are also eminently adaptable and will live happily in whatever style best suits their immediate environment. They are mainly herbivorous, but a number of species are omnivorous. They are prolific and breed up to five times a year, producing as many as fourteen young in each litter.

Rattus norvegicus, the brown rat, is found throughout the world. It is the largest of the common rats. It is known by various names: the grey rat, the house rat, the wharf rat, the barn rat. It is greyish brown in colour and dirty white on its underside. It causes considerable damage to food supplies and its fleas transmit diseases as deadly as typhus and plague. It is a fearlessly aggressive beast and will attack birds, animals, and man.

ANATOMY: from the Greek *anatemnein*, to cut up. A science of prehistoric age, anatomy deals with the structural organisation of living things. The earliest known study of anatomy dates from around 1600 BC and exhibits some knowledge of the greater organs but little understanding of their function. Some thirteen hundred years later, Aristotle would significantly further the science in regard to animals; major advances in the study of human anatomy were made in the third century BC by the Greek Herophilus, who dissected cadavers. There followed a lull in effective progress which lasted almost twenty centuries until the Flemish anatomist Vesalius, a son of the Renaissance, cast aside the paralysingly ancient texts that had been so long adhered to and began instead to base his learning on his own observations. The invention of the compound microscope in the seventeenth century revolutionised the science, allowing the study of tissue and cells. Legislation passed in the late eighteenth century restricting the use of human cadavers for medical research hampered the advancement of the science and heralded an age of such widespread body-snatching in England and the United States that the legislation was repealed in 1832. By the end of that century, most of the basic truths of anatomy had revealed their secrets. The science would grow infinitely more precise, infinitely more complicated, but, by the close of the nineteenth century, we knew what makes a living creature live.

⎯⎯

The rat on the table was dead. It seemed to Ravel the deadest thing he'd ever seen, that nothing had ever been deader. It lay on its back and was slit down the belly in a skilled, clinical way. Its skin had been neatly peeled away from the innards and was pinned back to a wooden board, three pins on either side, giving the rat a curiously tent-like appearance. Its tiny arms and legs had been drawn away with the flesh and this made the creature look desperate for an embrace. The gizzards had been loosened, uncoiled, wiggled apart, so all lay exposed within the confines of the tented skin and nothing was concealed as nature intended. The ribs and other bones, delicate as lashes, had been snipped as they intruded on the work, and placed at the bottom of a coffee mug.

Ravel knew what this was. He had dissected rats at school. Those rats had been frozen and sometimes imperfectly thawed, so pressure had to be put on the scalpel. Those rats were white rats, pink-eyed, bred for the purpose; the preserving liquid stained them a murky yellow. The rat before him was a grey rat, one of the hundreds that haunted the house. The hand that had held out food to this tame rat had then grabbed it by the scruff, broken its neck to stop the scrabbling.

Ravel looked around the room. Only a single candle burned, but the table was cluttered with dozens of candles, flecked with extinguished matches, and lumpy with fallen wax. Lit, these candles would illuminate the room as well as any electric globe. On the table, around the wooden block, lay Indigo's tools, each in its designated position. Scalpels of various sizes, scissors, tweezers, a small silver hammer for driving in the pins. Gloves for absent hands, a microscope, Bunsen burners cold for want of a gas outlet. On makeshift shelves were beakers and pestles, powders and fluids. Indigo had been stealing from all the laboratories he'd ever been in. On the floor was a birdcage, and this did not make sense until Ravel realised that the mess on the tray of the cage was made of rat droppings, rat urine, and scraps of food the rat had not wanted. This rat was a living experiment before it became a dead one. Ravel leaned closer.

The rat had a patch of blood smeared around its jaw. Its nose, too, was crusty with blood. Ravel picked up a scalpel and gave the innards a cautious prod. They moved sluggishly under the point of the blade. He brought the candle closer, the better to see. The gizzards looked damaged, to him: eaten, chewed. Gnawed. The smell of it made Ravel turn his face away.

The door had been open when he'd arrived. It rocked upon its hinges: there was always a breeze in the underground. Its source was untraceable; it was the breeze of ghosts, of happenings done. As children the twins had played hide-and-seek down here, in this creepy subterrain, and murder-in-the-dark. But Ravel almost never came here any more. This was Indigo's place, as the tower was Ravel's.

The door lurched and the candle flame swayed. The door of the birdcage was held open with a clothes-peg. The Kesbys had never owned a bird. The room was hazy with the fog of quenched flames, the door rocked and groaned. Ravel placed a palm on the back of the chair and found it warm. He ran his knuckles along the wicks of the unlit candles and they, too, were warm. Indigo came here: Indigo evidently spent a lot of time here. This room was a shrine, an operating theatre, a working laboratory: how warm was the rat?

The candle burning, the door swung back, the smell of magnesium sharpening the air: Indigo had only recently left the room. Indigo was coming back. Wherever he'd gone, he'd only gone for a moment. Ravel felt a shifty stab of panic. He knew, as one always knows, that this was not meant for him to see. Indigo had an inquisitive new hobby and it was evidently none of Ravel's business. He'd taken to chopping things into pieces and this was not, Ravel felt, quite sane. More than that, it was rank with menace. Ravel wavered: 'Indigo,' he whispered, 'what are you doing?'

Indigo kept secrets. He kept his brother secret and kept secrets from his brother. Ravel set the scalpel in its place and repositioned the candle. Then he left the room, just as he'd found it, and travelled through the labyrinth by the route Indigo was least likely to take, the route that led not into the house, but out of it.

In the garden, he resisted the urge to check if his twin was watching. He walked without haste to the place where his feet would find hold, and climbed the garden wall. He jumped down from it to the other side and snuck stealthily through the neighbour's territory, and away.

———

Indigo was playing the piano. He sat slightly hunched, his elbows hanging slack, the vitality concentrated into his hands alone. Attached to these energised, spiderish hands, the arms lurched back and forth the length of the key-board like something rolling with the sea waves. 'Shall I play you some Ravel?' he asked.

Ravel flopped into a chair and didn't answer. His feet

smarted, for the pavement had been hot. He was sunburnt on his calves and on the flesh between his shoulder-blades. He hadn't walked far: his exile from the day-lit world had left him shy of it, and he'd kept to the quieter streets. The cars made him apprehensive and he'd looked elsewhere until they had passed, and when he saw a child playing hopscotch on the footpath he'd crossed the road to avoid her. But he had walked determinedly: he would not be contained.

'Your dinner is in the oven,' Indigo said. His hands plucked out a dainty tune. 'It will need to be heated up. I'll do it for you in a moment.'

'Thank you.'

'I didn't think I'd wake you for it. Did you enjoy your sleep? Did you have a nice dream?'

'I wasn't asleep,' said Ravel.

'No? You're feeling better, then. That's good. I was getting worried about you. You've been a little ... *erratic*.'

'I've been for a walk, Indigo. You know that.'

Indigo did know it: he expressed no surprise and the tune did not slur or quicken in pace. But, 'You do many things without me now,' he said.

'Such as?'

'Everything.'

'Everything such as?'

Indigo frowned at the keyboard, but did not stop playing. 'Tell me,' he said, 'something about yourself.'

'Like what?'

'Anything.'

'Shall I tell you about the things I saw outside?'

'No. I don't care what you saw. I don't want to hear about what you do without me.'

'... Then I don't know what to say. Everything about me, you already know.'

Indigo chuckled and shook his ragged head. 'Oh, I doubt that,' he replied. 'I doubt that very much. Once I knew, but not any more.'

Ravel shifted in the chair, prising his legs from the grip of the leather. Indigo slowed his playing and eventually stopped. He closed the lid and looked at his twin.

'I'll tell *you* something, then,' he said. 'While you have been sleeping, I have been looking at our house. And I asked myself, Why is it, that this house has so many rooms? I'm sure there's rooms that we haven't even discovered, rooms that aren't yet real.'

'If they are there, they must be real,' countered Ravel. 'My answer is, I think the house has many rooms so a person could do something in secret, without another person knowing. So things can be done in private, and without interruption.'

Indigo never missed a beat. 'Ho ho!' he laughed. 'That's good, Ravel. That's nice and spooky and mysterious. That's better than the reason I thought up. I think the house has many rooms so a man can be king of a castle. A *castle*. You can't be king of a bed-sit. Or can you?'

'A small king, maybe. Anyway, I wasn't asleep. I told you that.'

'If you had been sleeping,' Indigo replied, 'you could have told me your dreams.'

'You would only tell me my dreams aren't real, like the rooms.'

Indigo sighed and dropped his hands to his knees. 'You know nothing about me,' he said.

'We know nothing about each other, then. How strange.'

'Someone came to the door and asked for you.'

Ravel went still. 'Who? Mrs Giotto?'

Indigo smiled sleekly. 'No, not her, not yet. Someone else. A girl.'

'A girl?' Ravel was taken aback.

'She asked me to give you this.'

Indigo unwound from his wrist a fine silver chain, a necklace, and dangled it from the tip of a finger.

'She said you left it at her house. She wasn't sure if it was a gift, or if you wanted it back.'

'I've never seen it before.'

'Yes you have. I have.'

'I'd remember –'

'I remember. I remember you showing it to me once. It came in a blue box. You thought it was pretty: perhaps she did not. She said she's been meaning to return it for a while, but she kept forgetting. She's shifting house at present and discovered it at the bottom of a drawer. So she brought it round. She thought I was you, and it was very awkward until I put her straight. I told her you were asleep, and that I didn't want you to be woken as you are unwell. Which is what I believed, at the time.'

Ravel stared at the swaying chain. He didn't remember it. He didn't remember a necklace or a blue box or a Mrs Giotto, and he wondered if he was going mad – or if it wasn't true. If what Indigo was saying wasn't true. If none of it was true, and Indigo was making it up. If Indigo was making it up.

'Did she say her name, Indi?'

'She did, but I knew it already.'

This was likely: even the house knew her name. Ravel tried, 'What did she look like? I mean, how did she look?'

'She looked well. She looked nondescript. A girl like any other. Short dark hair. Slight build. A pretty face. A face you'd find pretty, anyway.'

Ravel felt himself reddening, and looked at the floor.

It was a fair assessment of the girl he had adored, so long ago now that it seemed an attachment from another lifetime. A girl he'd believed he would have died for, whose rejection of him had caused him despair enough to wish his parents off the face of the planet.

'She can't have thought much of you,' Indigo added, 'if she's returning your gifts.'

Ravel, mute and crimson, scanned the carpet. He couldn't think, he didn't know what to think. His flesh felt embedded with needles. Had he given her a gift? He might have. In those heady days he would have given her anything, his heart, his eyesight, his parents on a platter. Everything had been extreme; the details were blurred then, and forgotten now. We forget what is important, in the end.

He surfaced slowly from spinning silence. 'I think I'm going mad,' he said.

'I don't think mad people know they're mad. But you might be.'

'Did she say where she was moving to?'

'No. My grief and embarrassment for you were such that I did not care to ask.'

Indigo spooled the chain in his palm and threw it at his brother. It hit Ravel's chest and dropped into his lap. It was warm, for something that should have been cool: being near Indigo had heated it through.

'If I were her, I would have sold it. Pawned it.'

'That isn't,' answered Ravel, 'the sort of thing she would do.'

'No? Well, you knew her.'

'Did she say if she'd come back?'

Indigo snorted. 'Ravel, she was returning your *presents*. I think that means she's well and truly *over* you.'

Ravel said nothing. Indigo stood up.

'Don't worry about it, Rav,' he said. 'She wasn't good enough for you.'

Indigo heated his dinner for him, and poured him a glass of milk, and later when Ravel confessed that his stomach hurt, that everything inside him hurt, his twin helped him undress and tucked him into bed and sat with him until he fell asleep.

THE ICY CLEARING

'Shall I tell you a dream of my own?' asked Indigo Kesby.

Ravel paddled his spoon through his breakfast bowl, the flakes of flattened corn sagging and resurfacing in the milk. 'If you like.'

'It was a weird dream, to have on a hot night. I was restless – as were you, I heard.'

'I wasn't feeling well.'

'I am not surprised. You look positively grey. You should try to eat your breakfast, though.'

'What was your dream?'

Indigo settled back into the kitchen chair. 'I was walking alone in a frosty wasteland,' he began, and with his hands he turned the table into a snowy tundra, and the bowls and the box of cereal and the milk jug ceased to exist. 'I had been walking there forever, it seemed to me quite aimlessly, but there must have been some purpose in my travelling, because my feet never hesitated. I tripped over sometimes, and sank in snow all the way to my chest, and hauled myself up more exhausted every time. Snowflakes were falling heavily and I couldn't see further than a few steps ahead of me. And then I reached a clearing, and I realised the clearing was made of ice. There was no snow on the ice: the surface was so clean and shiny that it reflected the sky, and the ice looked blue. The air was filled with loud, occasional sounds like the echo of a gun. It was the sound of the ice. It was the sound of ice that no longer wants to be ice.

'Far away, on the other side of the ice, I could see trees and the familiar blanketing of snow on the earth. Whatever force was driving me longed to be on that far side. I simply had to reach it, I thought I'd cry or die if I couldn't continue my journey. So I stepped out on the ice.

'I'd walked not the length of this room when the ice broke beneath me. I felt that horrible grip of horror, that pang in the heart that accompanies a dreadful truth. The ice caved in, and great slabs of ice were driven up as I went down. I grappled with them hopelessly as they, and I, plunged downwards. The water was over me in an instant and I saw myself, as one does in dreams, being sucked down in a swirl, the planks of ice coming with me, around me, closing the gap above me. The water was blue, and a million bubbles rushed up for the roof. It was cold – the coldest thing I've ever known – and I thought, I'm going to die. In a handful of seconds I will be dead.'

Indigo placed his chin in his hands and gazed thoughtfully at his twin.

'A good dream,' said Ravel.

'As dreams go, yes. As awful as it was, falling through the ice, that wasn't what woke me. You were.'

'I'm sorry. I had to have a drink.'

'It wasn't that,' said his brother. 'You didn't wake me by walking around the house. You woke me because you were under the ice, too. You were there before me. You were suspended in the water with your arms spread out

64

and your skin bleached white. And I knew – as if you'd spoken – that you had been there a very long time.'

Ravel lifted his eyes and stared across the table. Indigo quirked a perfect eyebrow.

'Yes,' he said. 'It was a weird dream.'

Ravel shoved his bowl away. 'I've had enough,' he said.

'Does your stomach still hurt? You should go to the doctor.'

'No.'

'Spend the day in bed, then.'

'No.' Ravel pushed out his chair. 'There's something I want to do.'

'Oh?'

'I'm going to visit that girl who gave you the necklace.'

Indigo gazed at his brother. 'You're not well,' he said. 'You shouldn't go out. You might have a fever.'

'I'm well enough.' Ravel smiled as proof. 'It wasn't far from here.'

'You'll get sicker,' Indigo promised darkly. He stepped from his chair and followed Ravel across the room. 'Anyway, she doesn't live there any more. She was shifting out, remember?'

'Shifting, not shifted. She could still be there.' Ravel took the house key from its hook and dropped it in his pocket. 'I'll give the necklace back, tell her it was a gift she was meant to keep. Tell her to pawn it, if she likes.'

'Ravel, I don't think you should –'

'I'll be all right. What are you worrying about?'

Indigo tightened his jaw. 'You don't believe me,' he said.

'. . . What?'

'You think I'm lying. You think I made the whole thing up.'

Ravel blinked. He scanned Indigo's face. 'I don't believe you about . . . what?'

Indigo glared. 'Go then,' he growled. 'Go, if you doubt me. Give the necklace back. Tell her you don't believe she exists while you're at it. Say you thought she was a lie. Don't bother to apologise when you find out the truth. I can live without your remorse.'

'Indigo?'

'She'll be glad to have it back, I expect. It must have cost Mother a fortune, after all. You've always been very generous – oh, except to Mother herself, that is. Not much generosity in that particular case. Couldn't stand her whining. Couldn't stand the sight of her. Had to be rid of her, of course.'

'That – that wasn't –' Ravel fumbled his retaliation. The day had been long, and it hadn't yet reached noon. His stomach was aching and skewing his concentration. 'That was a shitty thing to say,' he said.

'Oh, a thousand apologies!' Indigo cried. 'It's just that sometimes I get a little frantic around you, you see, wondering if I will be the next person to vanish from your life.'

'You wouldn't be,' Ravel replied. The ache of his stomach seemed to be contracting him, his arms and legs and insides, into a small, demanding, central point. He suffered, momentarily, one of the unfortunate side-effects of sickness – a decided apathy in regard to one's future. 'You wouldn't be,' he said. 'How could it happen? It's you who does the cleaning up after me. The fixer doesn't fix himself. The vanisher doesn't vanish.'

'What is *that* supposed to mean?'

'You know. Wherever did they go, Indigo?'

Indigo stepped forward and swiped his brother across the face. It was not a hard hit – just a gesture of frustration.

Ravel stepped back and gaped at him, uninjured, but startled.

'Ask me,' Indigo challenged. 'Ask me anything.'

The first drop of blood streaked Ravel's t-shirt, catching the attention of both twins. Ravel looked down at the splash of colour, garish against the whiteness of his clothing. Another drop fell, and another, a ruby necklace unstringing. Ravel tasted it as it ran from his nose and smoothed out over his lips. 'Jesus,' he muttered, and blood slid into his mouth, ringing around his gums. He put a hand to his nose and the blood pooled in his palm and splashed to the floor. Indigo stared as if mesmerised: it was moments before he was sufficiently collected to guide Ravel to his chair and clamp a tea-towel over his face.

'Sit forward,' Indigo instructed, but Ravel gasped and squirmed under his grip and wrenched the cloth away. He wrapped his arms around himself and slumped against the table-top. He could hear Indigo advising, apologising, his voice strained with the damage he'd done. He gagged and spluttered until the drops had flown everywhere, onto the floor, into their breakfast, over himself and his twin. The warmness of it, the taste and the thickness of it, was to Ravel the most revolting thing he'd ever known.

When he was able to sit back, sucking air through a mouthful of bubbles and slick, he felt dazed and weakly woozy, and sagged in Indigo's arms. Indigo, on his knees, held his brother close and dabbed Ravel's throat and chin. 'I'm sorry, Rav,' he whispered, and repeated it again and again. 'I'm sorry, I'm so sorry Rav, I'm sorry...'

Ravel rested; he felt almost bled to death. He closed his eyes and let his twin support him. Indigo wiped the blood from his hands and naked arms and the dry cloth caught at the drying droplets. Ravel sniffed and coughed and finally reached out a hand for his peppermint milk, and his lips left a red semicircle on the rim of the glass.

'Rav?' said Indigo. 'I think you'd better stay home.'

Ravel set his drink down and stared at it. He touched a finger to the bloodstain on the glass and left a smudged flesh pattern. 'Tell me,' he sighed. 'Tell me anything.'

'Anything?'

'Tell me something true.'

'A story?'

'Yes. A true story.'

'The story of the hobyans?'

Ravel smiled wanly. 'That's not a true story.'

'How do you know it isn't true?'

'I've never seen a hobyan.'

'And that means they don't exist? Ravel, I'm ashamed of you. They found an animal in the rainforest that they didn't know existed. It is like a deer, or an antelope. It has horns, which means it fights, which means it breeds, which means it survives. Was *it* not true, then, before it was found?'

'It's a . . . horrible . . . story.'

'No, it's a great story. It's a twenty-point story.'

'Tell it, then.'

Indigo settled down on the linoleum. 'An old man and an old woman lived in a cottage at the edge of a beautiful forest,' he began. 'They owned a big and courageous dog. The dog knew the forest was filled with sinister hobyans; the old man and woman didn't know hobyans existed.'

Ravel smirked, understanding the implications of this. His smirking was grisly, tinged with green and pink.

'One night the dog, with his keen ears, heard the hobyans creeping closer, closer, to the house. As a clawed hand reached up for the door handle, the dog began to bark. The hobyans, who feared nothing except dogs, scattered in terror. The old man, who was a woodcutter and liked his sleep at the end of the day, was roused furious from his bed, and cut off one of the dog's legs as punishment for the noise. The next night, the same thing happened again. Hobyans, barking, woken old man. Off went the dog's second limb.'

'Poor dog,' said Ravel. 'Poor two-legged dog.'

'The third night, the same. The hobyans crept close, close, dragging their sacks behind them. The dog, loyal despite the injustices inflicted upon it, hauled itself to its two remaining paws and roared: the hobyans fled screeching into the safety of the forest. The old man, unable to believe the animal had not learned its lesson, slew off the dog's third leg.'

'Ouch,' said Ravel. He rubbed his arms, where the blood had dried on his skin.

'The fourth night, hobyans approaching, dog fiercely barking, the dog loses its remaining leg. The hobyans, cowering in the undergrowth, are ravenously hungry by now. In their scratchy voices they hatch an evil plan. The following night the hobyans creep, creep, to the house. The brave dog hears them and howls until the floor starts to shake. The old man storms from the bedroom, wild with loss of sleep, and hacks off the dog's head.'

'Oh my God,' chuckled Ravel.

'The dog, now silent, cannot ward off the hobyans. They scurry up to the house and burst through the door. They bundle the old man and the old woman into the sacks and haul them back to the forest, where they cook them on the spit and eat them. They are yum. There's much frolicking in the forest that night. The end.'

'Well done.'

'It's worth more than twenty points, really.'

'Yeah, thirty, I think.'

The twins laughed. They liked their game where the score was forgotten and no one ever won. Indigo hugged his brother fondly, and patted him on the back.

'It was our dad who told it to us, wasn't it?'

'Probably. It is a Kasbah kind of story.'

'He liked to frighten us.'

'We liked to be frightened.'

'I miss him, sometimes.'

'Yes,' said Indigo, 'so do I.'

Ravel lifted his eyes and considered the face of his twin. 'Remember,' he said. 'Kasbah would put us in bed and tell us his stories. His stories, because he told them how he wanted to tell them. Goldilocks got sent to prison. William Tell missed the apple.'

Indigo smiled. 'He was warped.'

'Do you remember what happened with Romeo and Juliet?'

'God, yes.'

'Tell me.'

'Hold your nose, it's dripping again.'

'Indigo, remember?'

'How could I forget,' replied Indigo, 'the sight of the pair of them, swooning into oblivion on the dining-room floor?'

'They didn't get up, either.'

'Not until we'd begun to cry...Why did we cry?'

'We were only little.'

'Oh, yes.'

'Our tears resurrected them.'

'It was a fake knife, and fake poison ... it was a cruel thing to do to children.'

Ravel looked at the ceiling and at himself. He inspected his bloody flesh and clothing. He drew a deep breath before he spoke. 'I wonder,' he said, 'what stories

Kasbah could tell us now. What props, do you think, would he need?'

Indigo looked askance. Abruptly he said, 'Let me tell you something else – something else that is true.'

'What?'

Indigo touched a finger to the blood on the drinking glass, leaving an imprint of his own. 'Identical twins,' he said, 'have fingerprints that are almost indistinguishable from each other's. I think that comes from being so close during the time we were made. During the time we were skinned. Were given skin. Made our own skin, together.'

Ravel nodded, his eyes on the prints. 'If we died together,' he mused, 'if they found us here together, dead, they couldn't tell us apart by our fingerprints. Even dead, they wouldn't know which of us was which.'

'In death, as in life.'

'I could be buried under your name, and you under mine.'

'It wouldn't matter.'

Ravel looked sharply at his brother. 'Of course it would matter,' he said. 'It would matter. It would matter more than anything has mattered. While I'm alive, I don't have to be you. I can be Ravel if I want to be. If I was dead and buried under your name then I'd be Indigo, wouldn't I? To everyone who saw the stone, I would be Indigo. And I'd never be able to tell them otherwise. I'd be Indigo into eternity.'

Indigo looked wounded. 'Ravel,' he said, 'why do you try so hard to hurt my feelings?'

'I'm not trying to hurt your feelings. I just don't want to spend my life being you. What is the purpose of my being born, if I am you?'

'There's worse things, surely, than being mistaken for me?'

'There's not, Indigo, don't you see? You are Indigo –'

'And you are Ravel. We know it. What do you care if no one else does?'

Ravel groaned and pressed his hands to his face. 'I have to be,' he said, '*Ravel*.'

'But you *are* Ravel.'

'No I'm not! I'm nothing! I'm nothing!'

Indigo eased away from his twin. 'I don't complain,' he said, 'when I get mistaken for you. I don't feel like nothing.'

Ravel dug his nails into his eyes. 'You can't be me,' he whispered. 'I don't want to be you, and you're not allowed to be me. You're not me. Tell everyone that you're not me, and you never have been. Tell yourself, too.'

Indigo was silent for some time; Ravel did not drop his hands. Eventually Indigo got to his feet and walked around the table. Blood had flung into his breakfast bowl and made pearly pink puddles in the milk. He said, 'They thought about adopting you out, do you know? It's true. When you were a baby. It wasn't *you* they didn't want – they just didn't want *two*. But they never considered the idea seriously. They didn't act on it, obviously. They were worried about the effect it might have on me. They told me this, years ago. I promised I would never tell, but I don't like keeping secrets from you.'

Ravel squeezed shut his eyes. Indigo was a liar, liar, liar.

'I've always been grateful they didn't do it,' Indigo said. 'I wouldn't have wanted to live my life without you. And that's true, too.'

He pushed away from the table and headed for the door. 'I'm going out,' he said. 'I'm going to return the necklace. I'll have a shower and change my clothes and then I'll take the necklace back for you. I'll do it now, try and catch her before she moves away.'

Ravel said nothing, although Indigo waited.

'. . . Fine. You can have a shower after me. I won't use all the hot water.'

Ravel laid his hands on the table and spread his claggy fingers. 'You don't know where she lives,' he said.

'I do. If she hasn't shifted, I do.'

'You *don't*.'

'You've had her address in the book beside the telephone for two years, Ravel,' Indigo answered harshly. 'For some strange reason you haven't got around to crossing it out.'

———

. . . I have been thinking about repenting. What does that mean, to repent? My dictionary says it is to feel regret, contrition, etc., for what one has done or left undone, to think with regret or contrition *of*. The Bible, that wad of righteousness, wickedness, and everything in between, mentions the word *repent* (and its variations *repentance*, *repented*, *repentest* and *repenting*) on more than one hundred occasions. 'Yet if they shall bethink themselves in the land whither they were carried captives, and repent. . .' says the First Book of Kings, 'Then hear thou their prayer . . . and forgive thy people that have sinned . . .' Poor Job must do it hard: he swears he *abhors* himself, and repents 'in dust and ashes'. And the Revelation, which must have petrified the scribe St John out of his skin as it unfurled across his astounded mind, warns us to 'hold fast, and repent', for 'As many as I love, I rebuke and chasten: be zealous therefore, and repent'.

Why does the Bible squall so? Why does it feel such a need to *bully*? Who is it, after all, that does not *automatically* repent what he or she has done or left undone? Repenting is surely the most natural thing in the world. I wish I'd done this, I wish I hadn't done that: we say it or

73

think it a million times before we're through. It matters not a bit that repentance is futile, and alters nothing of what history has recorded and so irretrievably consumed. The Bible focuses on the repenting of *sins*, yet isn't it true that few of us (religious or not) wish to sin? We don't, most of us, want to hurt. We want to be good. We don't have to be *told* to repent, we just *do* it. It's a rare soul who rises brazenly above the inclination.

Indigo Kesby is such a rare soul. He said to Ravel, 'I'm sorry, I'm sorry,' but he wasn't sorry, not after he recovered (which he did with speed) from the initial shock of seeing the blood pour from his twin's nose. He was caught off-guard by the rapid effect of his experiment, and was somewhat overcome with the result. He made a mental note to reduce the dosage. But repentant? Oh no, I don't think so.

SOMEBODY MEANS BUSINESS

Indigo slotted his fingers in the space between the door and its frame and waited for Ravel to speak. His brother would have heard him swing the massive front door, drop the chain in its place and slide the bolt home. Ravel would have heard him shamble, still blind with the brightness of the day, to the kitchen, where he replaced the key on the hook and filled a glass of water for his thirst. He'd have heard his twin catch his foot under the hallway rug and swear, and he'd have imagined the whip of Indigo's hand, flung out to stop himself from tripping. Ravel would have heard and recognised the creak of each step when Indigo made his way up the pitch and narrow staircase, grumbling under the effort, stamping at the rats that scattered before him to show he was not in the mood for games. Indigo knew his brother's hearing was keen and he garnished many of his activities with unwarranted drama, for the benefit of Ravel's excellent ears.

But Ravel said nothing, did not invite his brother into the room, so Indigo pushed open the door and walked in. Ravel lay on his bed, sleeping, or dead. Indigo went to him and placed a hand on his chest.

'Ravel!'

Years ago, when he and Ravel were children, Indigo had enjoyed tormenting his brother as he drifted into sleep. 'Ravel!' he'd say, short and sharply, and Ravel would answer, 'Hmm?', always tilting the word to seem interested, ashamed of being asleep, pretending he was awake. Indigo would say, 'Do you want a chocolate?' or 'There's a spider on your face,' and Ravel, who could recognise nothing but his name in that state of teetering consciousness, wouldn't say or hear a thing. Indigo would play this game over and over until he grew bored. Ravel! – Hmm? – I'm much smarter than you – Nothing. Ravel! – Hmm? – I'm glad that you're my brother – Nothing.

Ravel's bedroom overlooked the rear garden from the third floor, but the curtain was drawn across the window. Ravel slept on a single bed and the room he chose to sleep in was a small one, comparatively, and set south, so at the best of times it received little light, yet it kept what warmth soaked into it, high up on the third floor with the treetops as a view. It was a cosy, dun-coloured, messy tinderbox of a room, strewn with a lifetime's memorabilia, and the overall effect was of a cocoon, cramped, warm, and brown. Ravel lay naked on his unmade bed, his fingers clutching a corner of sheeting, the book of a thousand tales splayed on the floor where it had been dropped. The heat and his illness made him perspire, and Indigo's hand came away from him damp.

'Ravel,' Indigo repeated. Ravel opened his eyes slowly, and found his brother without searching. Seeing this image of himself staring back at him, did he have to think, *That is Indigo: I am Ravel* – for the sake of clarity and assurance?

'What time is it?'

'It's six.'

'. . . Six?'

'Yes, six. It's evening.'

Ravel, still muzzy, glanced down the length of his body, and then around the room. He had not loosened his grip upon the sheet. 'I've slept all day,' he sighed. 'If it's six, I must have slept all day.'

'Shall I put the dinner on?'

Ravel shook his head. He tugged at the sheet weakly and it snagged under his weight. He had to arch his back and reposition his elbows before he could, with effort, draw the cover over himself. Indigo did not help him: Ravel's desire for privacy was, to him, mildly insulting. When are identical twins more identical than when they're in their birthday suits?

'Where have you been?' Ravel asked, once securely hidden. 'You said you wouldn't be gone for long.'

'I returned the necklace. I went to the bank. Other things. Time flew.'

'She took the necklace?'

'Yeah, she took the necklace.'

'Ah.'

'She'll be gone tomorrow. We caught her just in time.'

'Oh.'

'I told her how you doubted her existence,' Indigo said. 'She seemed to find this funny – after everything that has passed between you. I can't see what you saw in her, to tell you the truth. She's not nice. She's kind of weedy. All that fuss you made, I expected something better.'

Ravel said nothing. His dark eyes sought the book on the floor.

'Let's hope this is the last we hear of the ridiculous subject,' Indigo continued. 'You agree it's been ridiculous, don't you? It's led to a lot of embarrassing behaviour,

Ravel. I know you're sick, and I'd like to indulge you, but I really haven't the time or the inclination to play funny games.'

Ravel did not answer. He seemed to sink more deeply into his bed.

'How do you feel, anyway?'

'I have a headache.'

'I'm not surprised. Causing them, you'll get them. I have one too. It's been an awful day. I had to bring home bad news. Do you want to hear it now, or later? You might feel better later.'

'No,' said Ravel. 'I don't think I will. I'll get worse. I'm getting worse. It's only made a couple of moves: like chess.'

'Chess? I think you're delirious.'

'Do you? I don't know. Can I tell you something first?'

'What?'

'Give me the book.'

Indigo sighed and didn't hurry, but lifted the book from the floor.

———

The evening of Saturday, June 15th, 1822, found Robert Howe walking home. It was just after nine p.m. and the streets were dark and quiet. Robert was the publisher of the *Sydney Gazette*, and a decent and likeable man: he was on his way home, that night, after his regular visit to the local Mission-house, where he befriended the poor and the alone.

Robert walked without hurry, his mind elsewhere. His work at the *Gazette* occupied much of his thoughts much of the time. A man crossed the road and proceeded to walk six or seven steps ahead of him and although Robert was obliged to slow his pace, he thought nothing of it. Soon the man turned a corner and vanished. Robert was thinking about dinner now. He'd have something heartening: pork, or a big fish.

What happened, then, happened very quickly. As Robert reached the corner, the man pounced out from behind it and plunged a bayonet into Robert's chest. The publisher staggered backwards, astonished and bleeding copiously, and his assailant rushed away. The cry of 'Murder!' rang through the black streets and brought out the inquisitive, some of whom gave chase to the attacker. Night is an ally of the villain, however, and the mysterious man was never found.

Robert, meanwhile, reeled to a nearby doorway and hammered on the wood. His injury was deep and severe and he was, from all appearances, fast approaching death. Surgical aid was immediately summoned.

Robert Howe's life was saved. His lungs had narrowly escaped puncturing, as had all the major blood vessels. This was miraculous, given the size and the viciousness of the weapon used to inflict the wound. The bayonet was found abandoned on the street: it was a large and ancient blade, fastened to the end of a pole. It was mottled with rust and the fine edge had been hacked so the bayonet had the gnarling teeth of a saw. It was stained with a good deal of blood, having been driven almost four inches into Robert's chest. Somebody had meant business.

⌒

Ravel looked up at his brother. Indigo looked back blankly.

'What was the motive?' Ravel asked. 'Everyone wondered about the motive.'

'Journalists are notorious for offending their readers,' Indigo decided loftily. 'I'm surprised they don't get skewered more often.'

'How strange you should say that – listen to this.'

Ravel turned to the book and smoothed down the page. '"His only motive must have been REVENGE. The infatuated man must have long brooded over some fancied injury, till his passions were wrought into a frenzy, fit for the most ruthless deeds." How funny you guessed it was revenge. As opposed to wanton cruelty, for instance.'

'It smelt like revenge to me.'

'Did it? If it was revenge, the insult was imagined. Robert hadn't written anything damning about anyone for ages.'

'If it was revenge then he had done something, somewhere.'

'Nonetheless. A bayonet, with a carefully crafted spiky edge. You'd have to agree that's a most ruthless deed.'

Indigo licked his teeth. 'Revenge isn't something you should try to make sense of, Ravel,' he said. 'Revenge has a long tradition of getting carried away. It doesn't follow rules – there's no guidebook to revenge. That's the pleasure of it, you see. It's lawless. It doesn't need to equal the crime that caused it, because it is an innocent thing, it didn't bring itself to life – it's Frankenstein's monster, it's Medea's broken heart, it's a dog that's wicked only because it was encouraged to be that way. If I exact revenge, I may exact all the revenge I please, because I was blameless before you went out of your way to harm me.'

'What an interesting interpretation.'

'It was a good story. Ten points.'

'I don't want points.'

'Have them anyway. And now I'll tell you a story. May I sit?'

'Of course.'

Indigo pulled the chair away from the desk and sat

down. 'It's bad news,' he said. 'We're running out of money.'

Ravel looked up sharply. 'What? How? How can that happen?'

'It's simple mathematics. It's physics, it's chemistry, it's biology and geography. When you use a resource and don't replace it, that resource starts to shrink. Eventually it is all used up.'

'But I thought –'

'I thought so too. We thought wrong. The supply is not limitless. It isn't a stream or a river but a pool, and it's getting mighty shallow. At the moment we have enough to last four or five months.'

'But that can't – that can't be. That money was invested, it was earning interest, it should have got bigger, not smaller –'

'God, Ravel!' yelped Indigo. 'You know everything, do you? Here in this room, in this house, you somehow know everything. Who does the banking, huh? Who has always done the banking?'

'. . . You.'

'So who would know best about the matter?'

Ravel looked sullen and didn't reply. Indigo gave him a chilly smile. 'You're quite welcome,' he said, 'to go to the bank and inspect the account yourself. Half of it is yours, after all. Annie and Kasbah seemed to think you expected them to leave *it*, as well as us.'

Under his sheet, Ravel breathed heavily. His chest was weighted. His stomach felt as if it had developed a small puncture, through which was leaking gore. The thought of running out of money made his heart stand still. He was frightened: he'd been frightened for days. Once he'd just been harmlessly bored, and now he was utterly terrified. Giving voice to his boredom had loosed a monster. 'What are we going to do?' he asked.

Indigo shrugged, and looked round the room. On the shelves were books and toys, feathers, sticks and leaves. Propped on the top shelf, close to the ceiling, perched a rat that Indigo momentarily believed to be stuffed, until it moved. It lifted a paw and placed it down again, as if acknowledging its reflection in Indigo's eyes. 'I don't know,' he said.

'We'll have to do something.'

'Obviously.'

'What? What?'

'We should regard the problem as a blessing – it won't hurt so much then. You know I don't like paying bills.'

Ravel stared at his twin. 'No,' he muttered, 'you can't do that . . .'

'I don't see what else can be done.'

'Indigo, you can't! What will we cook with? We need hot water! You can't do it!'

'We would survive.'

'I could not survive like that!'

'You'd die if you couldn't have a hot bath, would you?' Indigo smiled. 'Dear me. That would be dying of sheer pique.'

'Indigo, please – don't –'

'Have you got a better idea?'

Ravel forced himself to sit up. The exertion made his mind swirl. 'I'll get a job,' he said. 'I'll go looking tomorrow, I'll do anything, it doesn't matter, I told you I wanted one –'

'I remember. But what you want is a doctor. You're not going anywhere tomorrow.'

Ravel shook his head, close to tears. 'Please, Indi,' he begged. 'Don't. I couldn't bear it. I couldn't.'

Indigo rolled his eyes. 'Cavemen lived without gas, you know.'

'Oh, God . . .'

'It doesn't seem to have hampered them. Look at the world: grossly over-populated, yet the gas-fuelled stove is a comparatively recent invention. Our lives would continue with only the slightest –'

A tear dropped down Ravel's face and brought his twin to a silent halt. Ravel put a hand to his eyes and smeared away those that might follow. His hand, Indigo noted, was shaking, and his colour was definitely grey. There was not much fight left in him now. Indigo moved to the bed and put an arm around him.

'Stop it,' he said. 'Don't cry, Ravel. I'm sorry if I frightened you. I'll think some more before I decide anything. But it's not something that can be put off forever, do you understand? This problem is not going to fix itself.'

Ravel nodded, his face hidden in Indigo's shirt. 'Thank you,' he whispered.

'Don't thank me yet.'

'Thank you,' Ravel repeated doggedly, so pathetically grateful that Indigo felt quite touched. He tilted Ravel's chin and put a finger to his lips.

'Be quiet,' he said. 'Don't worry.'

Ravel, hushed, gazed at his brother and saw his face, twice: Indigo's version, imperceptibly finer than his own, and, in Indigo's eyes, his own face, anxiously drawn. Ravel's world was a looking-glass: whenever he looked, what he saw was the same. Indigo smoothed away a fall of his hair and it swung, scythe-like, back again.

'Lie down,' he said. 'You're sick and upset. I want you to rest.'

Ravel lay down. Indigo tucked the sheet around him and sat back, considering him. 'You're silly,' he said, and flicked his brother on the nose. 'You're really silly, aren't you?'

Ravel smiled lamely, and hoped his nose would not start to bleed again.

'You are.' Indigo stood, and dusted his hands. 'I'll get dinner started,' he said.

'Don't cook for me, I'm not hungry.'

'All right. I'll bring you a glass of milk and a tablet for your headache.'

'It wouldn't be so bad,' Ravel said abruptly, 'if you'd noticed it before.'

Indigo turned. 'Noticed what?'

'Noticed that the money was going down. If you'd noticed it earlier, it wouldn't be so bad. It wouldn't have come so . . . suddenly.'

'I must be even sillier than you,' Indigo replied. 'I am silly – I've forgotten something. Your girly friend gave me this to give to you.'

He drew an envelope from his pocket and tipped the contents into his palm. A lock of mousy hair, bound with a band and a red ribbon, coiled itself across his hand. Ravel's eyes widened at the sight. It was exactly the right colour, exactly the right curl. Indigo lifted it by the ribbon's loop and danced it from a fingertip.

'Horrible, isn't it?' he remarked. 'I do hate the touch of other people's hair. There's something so . . . *hormonal*, about it. Still, there you go. Not only proof, but a keepsake as well.'

He dropped the lock on the bedside table but then, evidently finding this placement unsatisfactory, he moved the hair further away, to the desktop, where Ravel could not easily see it. 'So there,' he said smartly. 'Will that be one tablet or two?'

Indigo took the cloak from its hanger and bundled it into a black mass. When he pressed the material to his face he could smell the lingering odour of his mother's occasional cigarettes. He laid the cloak down and bowed to it. 'The music begins,' he whispered. 'May I ask for this dance?'

He arranged the cloak against his body so the hem brushed his shins and the collar lay over his shoulder. It formed a lithe and free-moving partner for him then, its pose a doting swoon. He twirled around his parents' bedroom and the cloak swept after him fluidly, gusting dustballs over the carpet. 'You dance like a dream, my dear,' Indigo murmured in its ear. 'What is that perfume you wear tonight? Nicotine? How divinely naughty of you.'

He closed his eyes, dipped, spun. As the music in his head reached its peak he danced with more and more abandon, crashing off the cupboard and the walls. At the crescendo of kettledrums and blaring horns he took his hand from the small of the cloak's back and the material soared out over the room. A box of tissues that had sat untouched on the dresser for a year and a half was instantly knocked flying and the noise made Indigo stagger to a stop. He frowned at the dented box, and at the limpen cloak. 'I do believe you're drunk,' he said.

He shook out the garment and settled it around his shoulders. The satin lining was pleasant against his bare skin, and cool. He went to the mirror and paced up and down before it. Something was missing. His mother had hats in boxes under the bed and he rummaged through them until he found one that was coloured an appropriate gold. It had a bow around the brim, and this he removed with nail scissors. He cut the brim itself off, and then he punched the scissors through the top of the hat. The felt made a gratifying *pop*. He trimmed and carved until the hat became a circle of angles: a crown. He sat it on his head and returned to the mirror. Better. Annie had owned a good deal of jewellery but Indigo had sold the best pieces long ago. He was forced to rifle through the worthless remains but found necklaces and bracelets that were good enough for the purpose. Returning to the mirror, he was satisfied he looked like a king.

That night Indigo thundered through the house, leaping, romping, capering. He was the first-born son, the prince, the lord, the heir. Everything to own was rightfully his, and this was his domain. He slid along banisters and did cartwheels in the hall. He pranced and galloped and sprang. The furniture was delighted by his jubilance and shuffled close to be clambered on. He wrestled chairs to the floor and bounced upon the couch. The objects grovelled around him, pleading for a touch of his magnificent hand. They lined up eagerly to sacrifice themselves. He threw ornaments in the fireplace and books across the rooms. He smashed the plates he'd eaten from and stomped the shards into the carpet. Anything he wanted, he allowed himself to do.

Upstairs, at the opposite end of the house, Ravel lay on his bed and stared at the shadowy ceiling. He could hear Indigo like a tiger within the house, but he lay as still as he could. He ached, if he moved. But Indigo would be tedious if he didn't finish his glass of milk: wearily Ravel reached out for it, and swallowed the last of the tepid remains.

YOU'LL GET NO MUSICK FROM ME

Ravel closed the book and let it rest upon his chest. The weight of it seemed to calm and suppress the wrenching of his stomach. He had no idea what time it was, having no clock, no need for a clock, but the streak of sunlight powering its way through the small gap in the curtain told him it must be daytime, mid-afternoon. The light stung his eyes and he kept away from the places where the invasive brightness touched the bed. He did not know how the day had passed for him, although he supposed he had slept through much of it. The pain let him sleep in fits and starts, as if to give him energy for withstanding its next attack. It occurred to Ravel that he wasn't certain what day it actually *was* – Monday? Thursday? – and he contemplated this gap in knowledge and memory for a short while before casting it, too, into the apathetic abyss. He stroked the book's papered cover with his fingertips and hummed a dull tune to himself.

There were rats in Ravel's bedroom. Mostly they stayed between the walls, but occasionally one or two would venture out to lick the plates that Ravel had eaten from and Indigo had not yet come to collect. They dabbed the crumbs up swiftly and when they had finished they would conduct sniffing searches of the empty plates, certain something had been overlooked. They drove their snouts under the rims of the plates, using their skulls for leverage, and scoured the floorboards beneath. They tipped the glasses deftly and made quick work of the pools of peppermint milk. When they were convinced they'd found everything there was to be gained, they would crouch and look dissatisfied and they'd turn their tiny eyes then, upwards, to Ravel.

Indigo Kesby was exasperated by the behaviour of the rats. He had thought of them, at first, as *his* rats, but their behaviour so frustrated him that he had reduced their status to *the*. The rats appeared willing to do nothing but sit in the birdcage and wait for themselves to die. What had Indigo been expecting? Theatrics. He'd wanted reeling, stumbling, thrashing. For some reason he had thought they would *fight*. But the two rats, as similar as twins but not identical twins, for one had a smattering of white within its grey, simply sat, disinclined to even blink. If there were death throes going on anywhere they were going on in private, and Indigo felt himself, as a scientist, sorely denied. He slid the blunt end of a scalpel through the bars of the cage and prodded the mottled rat in the ribs. It flinched, and shifted its position a fraction. It settled closer to its twin and closed its eyes. Indigo slumped in his chair and crinkled his nose. At least Ravel was proving more interesting than this.

It seemed important to Ravel that he should not languish in his room forever. He didn't know what day it was. Nothing happened for hours. The silence had become traumatic. The big house was by nature a communicative thing, its frame carrying messages from its depths to its roof. It spoke about itself in creaks and groans. It spoke about the life within it: it reported the dropped saucepan, the tumbling desk-lamp, the amusement or crossness of those in the furthest room. And for hours, for as long as he'd been aware he was listening, it had been silent, and Ravel was afraid he'd been left alone.

'Indi,' he called, in the hallway. 'Indigo?'

He had to walk with his arms around his waist, as if his illness demanded affection. His legs could only shuffle: to lift his feet and bend his knees sent pain yowling through his intestines, and the staircase had been an everest of agony down which he'd hopped and slid. He was moving like a cripple, or an alcoholic. It took a long time to get anywhere.

It was important to speak to Indigo. Indigo had the run of the house. He seemed to have the run of the world. How many days had Ravel slept through – Monday? Monday until Thursday? And Indigo would not have sat still. His busy little mind would have been ticking, ticking. He was not to be trusted: he was rash, and lacked prudence. He had to be found, and when he was found he had to be told that this was a momentary lull in Ravel's vitality and would soon enough be overcome. This was no time to take advantage, decisions should not be made in Ravel's name or absence, everything that was done should be fair. *Consider the future*, is what Ravel wanted to implore of Indigo, and what repeated in his mind as a mantra until it lost all its slimmest meaning.

The house, downstairs, was cooler, but the windows were shut and most doors had been closed. It gave the house the unmistakable feeling of vacantness, abandonment. Ravel stood worried by the sight, chewing at his fingernails, muttering his brother's name. The thought of being alone distressed him to an unreasonable degree. He could not pinpoint the last time he'd seen Indigo. He had not kept track of the meals his brother brought to the bedroom, had no idea if they arrived with any regularity. He couldn't remember his last meal. It was always the same meal, buttered toast and flavoured milk, and individual occasions were melded into one. If Indigo was gone, he might have been gone for days.

In the kitchen Ravel startled a rat that was biting determinedly through a box of rat poison. It fled to the edge of the table before collecting itself, and turned to give Ravel an angry stare before leaping off the table and skittering behind the stove. Three boxes of poison were lined up on the table but the rat had chosen to ignore the two already opened and easily raided. Evidently it felt it must work towards its own demise. Indigo said they were smart, these rats, but Ravel was not convinced.

There were dishes in the sink but it was hard to tell how long they'd been there. The kettle was more reliable: if it had been used that day it would hold its heat within its iron walls, and when Ravel touched it it was reassuringly warm. The warmth meant Indigo was still around; it also meant Indigo had not yet disconnected the gas supply, and Ravel felt woozy with a simpleton's joy. He poured himself a glass of water and sat down to wait.

The boxes of rat poison were coloured glossy green, an unbefittingly vibrant colour for a box of something lethal. They were neat, tough little boxes and bore the image of a rat — not a rat chomping rat poison but a rat just sitting and staring dreamily into space. The brand-name was printed in big letters, but the word WARNING was written quite small. KEEP AWAY FROM CHILDREN AND PETS. WASH HANDS AFTER USE. DO NOT CONSUME. Beside the words was a little skull and crossbones, as if rat poison was the realm of pirates. Ravel slid an open box across the table, to read the list of ingredients. The box was lighter than he'd expected: it skidded off the table and onto the floor. When he picked it up and rattled it, it made no sound. He tried the other open box, tipping it over with a finger. The rat he'd startled was not so stupid after all: it had gnawed through the unopened box because it was the only box, of the three, that had anything inside it. Green pellets, which were making a pile on the table as they escaped, one by one, from the tattered hole in the cardboard.

'I'm sick of the sight of them,' said Indigo, and took the seat opposite his brother. 'They make the house smell. I've embarked on a campaign of eradication.'

'. . . I'm glad.'

'You shouldn't be. You have something in common with the rat.'

'I smell?'

'You're secretive. What are you doing, creeping about? Are you spying on me?'

'No. I was looking for you.'

'Why?'

'Because –' What reason was acceptable? 'Because you're my twin.'

Indigo smiled. 'Yes,' he agreed. 'Indigo.'

Ravel returned the smile gingerly. 'You're looking . . . stately.'

Indigo preened the cloak so it sat more gracefully around his shoulders. 'I'm rather taken with it myself. It's bloody spiffy.'

'It's mother's, isn't it?'

'No, it's mine.'

'Oh.'

'Should you be out of bed?'

'I wanted to talk to you.'

'About? Hurry.'

'I don't remember.'

'Your brain might be damaged.'

'I feel a bit better.'

'It probably won't last.'

'Look at you. You look worse than I feel.'

'I do, do I?' Indigo laughed, without mirth. His eyes were ringed with violet, as if the colour had leaked from the irises. His hands, which lay on the table with the fingers tightly entwined, were blotched with grime. Under the cloak he wore only boxer shorts, and his chest was streaked in the places where he'd wiped these grubby hands across it. 'I feel great,' he said. 'I bet I know what you wanted to talk about.'

'Well?'

'You're worried about the money, aren't you? You've been turning the matter over in that damaged old head of yours, haven't you? I could hear it. I could hear you thinking.'

'You were right: the problem will not fix itself.'

'No indeed it will not. I'm pleased to hear you say so. I thought you might continue to deny its existence.'

'I never denied its existence.'

'Yes you did. You said it *couldn't be.*'

'It's surprising when something that shouldn't happen happens. *Assuming* there is a problem, it's in my interests to think of a way to fix it. A way that suits both of us. Two minds are better than one.'

Indigo made no sign of agreement to this. 'What is your solution, then?'

'I was thinking,' said Ravel, 'that we should sell the car.'

'Sell the car? What would we do if we wanted to go for a drive?'

'We never want to go for a drive.'

'But if we *did*. No, we're not selling the car. No. No no no. It's quite out of the question.'

Ravel nodded patiently. 'In that case, we could sell some of the furniture. We could sell everything. We need gas more than we need candelabras.'

His twin smiled. 'What an interesting idea,' he said. 'We could have a garage sale and serve tea to the neighbours. Little stickers for the price-tags. That would be a lot of fun. But the gain from it would be temporary, wouldn't it? We'd run out of furniture and fittings soon enough and then we'd be back in the same difficult position – only worse, because we'd have nothing to sit on while we suffered. Not to mention the shock it would be to Annie and Kasbah when they come home, seeing the house stripped bare.'

Ravel said nothing. He looked at the empty boxes of poison. Indigo lounged across his chair.

'Anyway,' he purred, 'I've fixed the problem already. It's not that I don't appreciate your suggestions, but I think my solution will be best in the long term.'

He stopped, forcing Ravel to look at him.

'I'm going to get a job,' announced Indigo. 'It will be a change, and a sacrifice for us both, but there you are, there's not much else that can be done. It will mean I'm gone for most of the day, but we'll get used to that. You might even become accustomed to your solitude, and get up to all sorts of mischief in my absence. To tell the truth, Rav, I'm looking forward to it. It's time to get out and see something different. And it will be nice, coming home each day to find you waiting for me, and a decent meal laid out on the table.'

Ravel stared at his brother, speechless. How does it feel, to be *speechless*? Ravel felt like he'd been gutted, gouged painlessly clean.

'But – Indigo –'

'But nothing, Ravel. The decision is made. I'll survive, and so will you. You're pliable, tractable. I'll get a good job, too. Nothing pissy or boring. Forensic science, perhaps. I've got a feeling I'd be good at that. I've got a hankering to get back into a handsome white laboratory coat. Or maybe a gangster. I've always fancied gangsterism as a career. A gag and a gun. What think you?'

Staggered, Ravel took his gaze from his brother and fixed it firmly on the table-top. Enfeebled already, he sensed he should not squander his strength on a pointless display of fury. He lifted his head and smiled charmingly at his twin. 'I didn't come here just to talk about the money,' he said. 'I came to tell you a story.'

Indigo was fanning his face with the hem of the cloak. 'Go on,' said he.

———

In 1798 nineteen Irishmen were passed into the custody of Sydney jail, the charge against them being that of *rebellion*, rebellion enough to endanger the security of His Majesty's Government. The Government wanted Information and the method best suited to procuring information was torture – in this instance, whipping. The whippings were elaborately arranged, involving a large tree and two practised floggers, one left-handed, the other right, stationed on either side of the prisoner's back and each armed with a cat-o'-nine-tails. Witness accounts state that spectators needed to stand at a distance or be splattered with the flesh the twin cats tore from the bodies tied to the tree. The tree was carefully chosen for size and broadness, and the prisoner was bound flush to

94

it with his arms hugging the trunk: this way, a man was unable to cringe.

It was illegal, at that time, for a prisoner to receive more than fifty lashes without a doctor being present. On this occasion the men were to get three hundred lashes each and a doctor was indeed present: Doctor Mason. Doctor Mason would inspect the sagging victim from time to time and he would smile and say, 'This man will tire you before he will fail – go on.' And the floggers would go on. They lashed the Irishmen mercilessly but the Irishmen were tough, used to tough lives, and not a word could be got from them. One man, whose name is recorded as Morris Fitzegarrel, took his three hundred cuts without saying anything except, 'Don't strike me on the Nick, flog me fair.' Fitzegarrel must have been a bullock of a man: when two constables freed him from the tree and led him to the hospital cart he gave both officers a crippling elbow to the guts and then stepped, cool and unaided, into the cart. Doctor Mason, watching and impressed, was heard to remark, 'That man had strength in nuff to bear two hundredd more.'

Paddy Galvin was up next. He was only twenty years old but he would receive three hundred lashes, like the rest. The first hundred laid bare his spine. Doctor Mason ordered the next hundred to strike the boy's flanks. These reduced the flesh to jelly. The doctor directed the final hundred to find the calves of Galvin's legs. These left nothing to hold the boy upright. But Galvin didn't whimper throughout the ordeal, and when they let him loose and hauled him up he said, 'You may as well hang me Now, for you will never get any musick from me.'

— ◦ —

Ravel smiled. 'You'll get no music from me.'

Indigo said, 'I'm getting tired of your stories.'

'Don't you find it interesting, that punishment can be pointless?'

'Punishment proves an awareness of the crime, while giving the punisher some satisfaction.'

'It got nothing in this case. The punishers looked like fools. Those men were true.'

'True to their piddling convictions, I suppose you mean? And you admire that, do you?' Indigo leaned forward, his cloak like wings around him. 'Do you know what flogging does to a man, Ravel? It *flays* him. It *tears* the skin from him. When the flesh is gone it tears, instead, through the muscles. It breaks the bones that become exposed. Those that didn't bleed to death died from infection in excruciating pain. Those who somehow survived took months to heal and were never the same again. That's not being true to yourself. That's stubbornness beyond the point of idiocy.'

'You think it's idiocy, to die for an ideal?'

'Of course.'

'You are wrong.'

'I don't think so. An ideal is just an idea that's run up against a wall and solidified in old age. It's better to be adaptable than idealistic. It makes life easier.'

'If what I want is all I want, what's the use of living without it? I will fight to the finish to get what I want.'

'Your death would be a waste. There's nothing worth dying for.'

'Freedom?'

'Oh, please. *Freedom*.'

Ravel laughed hopelessly, shaking his head. 'You cannot – you *will never* – make me agree. You could kill me, but you wouldn't have won.'

Indigo gave him a silky smile. 'It's romantic of you to believe otherwise,' he said, 'but being dead is very different from being free. Don't try for a hollow victory, Ravel: it's impossible to beat something stronger, something infinitely more determined, than you will ever be.'

The warning, spoken smoothly, rushed at him like a pack of wolves, but Ravel stood his ground. 'It's been nice having this talk with you,' he said.

'Yes, I've enjoyed it.'

Ravel hesitated. He wanted to be with his brother, inside his brother, digging a rusty nail into his brother's side. He wanted to raise the hair on Indigo's neck, to shake the ground under his feet. Indigo shot a glance at him, dark-eyed and defiant.

'I bought some bath salts for you,' he said. 'They're supposed to make you relax. Or soothe you. Or something. They smell nice.'

Ravel went to speak, and said nothing. His stomach hurt, and now his heart hurt. Indigo had been his hero, and still was. Once, when they were children, Indigo was given Superman for Christmas, and Ravel got inferior Aquaman. Seeing Ravel's disappointment, Indigo did something that was so characteristic of him: he swapped the toys and never referred to the incident again. He would politely ask for permission to borrow Superman. Ravel adored Indigo, and his heart hurt: he muttered, 'Thanks.'

'They probably don't work.'

'Thanks anyway. I will – I'll have a bath.'

'Now? Do you need help?'

'No. You stay there.'

Indigo stayed seated. He watched his twin hobble to the door. And then he asked, 'Ravel, what have you been doing to yourself?'

Ravel stopped in the doorway. 'What?'

'Your back looks funny. The backs of your legs look funny. Stand still, let me see.'

Ravel craned his head in an effort to watch while Indigo inspected him, pressing his fingers gently to the flesh. 'Does that hurt?'

'Not really.'

'I've never seen anything like it.'

'What is it?'

'Bruises,' Indigo marvelled. 'You're covered in bruises. They're all over you. As far as I can tell, you're well on your way to becoming one gigantic bruise.'

'Bruises? Where did they come from? What are they doing?'

'They're not doing anything. They're just smiling at me. I can't believe you couldn't feel them. They're the colours of the rainbow. They're really pretty.'

'Oh God, Indi, don't laugh, this isn't funny. You've got to take me to the doctor. I think it's time to go to the doctor.'

'Yeah, stop squawking. I'll ring and make an appointment for tomorrow.'

Ravel nodded, quelling panic. 'Don't forget.'

'I'll go to the phone booth while you're having your bath.'

When his twin left the room Indigo resumed his seat at the table. He listened to the sound of Ravel filling the bath, and while he listened he played with a box of rat poison. He heard Ravel step into the bath and he made himself wait several laborious minutes more, just to be sure. Then he swooped across the room, grabbed the tools and the bolt from where he'd hidden them under the sink, and dashed lightly up the stairs. When he reached Ravel's bedroom door he made quick and accurate measurements, made marks with a sharpened pencil. He tapped a nail into the door and wriggled it free again. He took a screw-driver and twirled a screw into the shallow nail-hole and twirled it out again. Six times he did this, leaving four scarcely visible cavities in the door and two in the dark wood of its frame. Kasbah had an electric drill (scarcely used and soon to be pawned) and it would have been fun to use it for the job, but refusing to pay bills means having to make the occasional sacrifice.

THAT IS NOT A LEGITIMATE REASON

Ravel is standing on the edge of a glass pane. On the edge of a grassy plain. No, a glassy plain. Windows must melt, for surely this is ice. He steps out onto it and he walks ten paces before a fissure opens beneath his weight. The single crack becomes a maze of fractures, with him at its centre like a spider in a web. The moment of the shatter is gratifying: he's longed for the moment, dreamed of it. He's prayed to be under the ice.

Mrs Giotto is not real, but she kisses him. 'Wavel,' she coos, 'Wavel.' She wraps her arms around him and clasps him to her swollen stomach. The hump beneath her dress writhes and kicks at him. He struggles to escape her grip, his feet skidding on the grass. She sets him free and he falls, the earth thumping air from his chest. 'Sweet Jesus,' moans Mrs Giotto. 'Sweet Saviour Jesus.' A piglet lands on the ground between her feet and immediately runs for Ravel. Its gait is lurching, for it lacks a limb, and its mangled face means it is blind.

Ravel finds rooms that aren't true, having never existed. He weaves through this jumble, at every corner catching glimpses of a hand that beckons and warns him away. He cannot match its silken speed and he asks the hand to wait for him, but it leaves him far behind. He hears the wailing of things that are lost.

There are goblins hung on scaffolds in a city he does not know, and fish flapping on the bitumen. Ravel, lost too, rushes through the streets, calling frantically for Indigo.

'What is it?' asks Indigo. With one hand he plays the piano. His arm is thin and flexible as a rubber band. The hand at the end of it is broad and flat as a plate.

'The doctor,' pants Ravel. 'Wasn't I supposed to go to the doctor?'

'The doctor came to you,' Indigo replies. 'He diagnosed a bout of ratiocination.'

'Ratiocination? What is that?'

'It is the reason why you are turning into a rat. It's genetic, you know. Annie and Kasbah turned into rats too.'

Indigo brings his hands to his face and his fingers make whiskers that wiggle: he giggles. Ravel clutches the door frame, fearing he might faint.

'Indigo, help me, I don't want to be a rat –'

Indigo laughs louder, his whiskers growing long.

'Indigo! Indigo!'

'What is it?' asks Indigo snappily. 'Open your eyes, Ravel: what is it?'

Ravel's eyelids flutter and he looks up at his twin. 'We're going to the doctor today, aren't we?'

Indigo sighs. 'That was two days ago,' he says. 'The doctor came to you. She said you had some stupid virus.'

'I don't remember.'

'So what? Go back to sleep. And if you're going to call me all the way up here, at least have the courtesy to be awake when you do so.'

⤙

Ravel woke, clear-headed. He recognised his room and knew why he was in it. He had no idea how much time had passed since he'd talked in the kitchen with Indigo, and suspected it might be days. His bed and body were damp, the sheets stained with crimped patches. He wondered if this was sweat, or if he'd wet the bed. It was difficult to tell if the heat was in the room or his body.

Nothing hurt inside him. The spearing pains had levelled out to become a hovering, flattening weakness. He understood this as a symptom of finality: he was not getting better, but worse. The illness had dug itself painfully in: now that it had a place to exist it could work like a craftsman, rather than a labourer. Ravel realised he was going to die, and he accepted this with graceful resignation.

The human brain is capable of producing substances known as endorphins, which have a morphine-like effect upon the body. It is possible that the ability to make endorphins developed in us when we were living in uncivilised times: the caveman facing a beast intent on consuming him was served better by composure than by frenzied panic. Endorphins are released by the brain in times of stress or trauma, and their purpose might be to alter emotional reactions and to lift the threshold of pain. They may enable us to deal with pain and fear by draping over us a sense of dispassion, even tranquillity: it could be endorphins which allow us to function in the face of emergencies that should otherwise render us rigid, and endorphins which let some die wearing an expression of serenity, despite dreadful circumstances. Endorphins, then, may protect us from actions that could lead to death and, when death is inevitable, cushion us against the horror and agony, so death is relatively peaceful. Endorphins kicked in on Ravel, rendering him untroubled. He accepted the natural poetry in being born, in living, in conceding one's place to another. He felt not the smallest objection to dying so young and so inexplicably. He looked around his room with great kindness in his eyes. He wanted to thank the objects that had decorated his life, the little bed that had supported him, the rug on the floor that kept his feet warm. He saw a poignant beauty in everything – the sunlight's persistent nosing for a break in the curtain, the small ticking sound the rats made when crossing the room. The rats had the sweetest faces: tiny round eyes comically bulbous, ears like coins lying flush against their heads. Rats keep their coats perfectly groomed – they value themselves, if no one else does.

The floor of the bedroom was jumping with rats. Indigo had been bringing meals that Ravel hadn't eaten, and the rats had congregated in this place of bounty. They scattered for cover when Ravel turned his head toward them, but soon felt secure enough to return. They roamed about on aimless missions, their long bodies zigzagging the floor or skimming along the walls. When their paths crossed they reared and briefly battled, emitting rapid squeaks. Ravel guessed there must be twenty or more within the tight confines of his bedroom. If there were rats enough for the same number to occupy every room of the house, there must be nearly three hundred of the creatures. Three hundred prepared to make themselves visible, and three hundred more that no one ever saw: rats that haunted the garden, the attic, the cellar, rats that took chicks from their nests beneath the eaves. For all the rat poison Indigo was going through, it was having scant effect on the rats.

Rat poison contains a drug called warfarin. Warfarin is a blood-thinner: in medicine it is used to treat patients who have clots or thrombosis. Used as a poison, warfarin's effects are similar to and easily mistaken for a vitamin K deficiency – lack of this vitamin hampers the blood's ability to clot. When blood is thinned by warfarin, the sufferer is prone to haemorrhaging. The lightest blow causes the capillaries to rupture into the surrounding tissue; as the blood absorbs, it leaves the discoloration of a bruise. The smallest tear in the skin will cause an inappropriate amount of blood to escape while the body endeavours to form a clot. Warfarin, used in doses high enough, leads to internal bleeding, and it is this that kills off rats.

Ravel, sensible under the influence of his endorphins, thought carefully. He lifted an arm and the rats raced off like mercury. His forearm was black: he rested his head on his arm while he slept. In the bath he had knocked his kneecap against the tap: he drew the knee up and was dazzled by the blueness of the blemish there. He thought about his headaches, and the crippling ache of his stomach. He thought about the way his nose had bled the day Indigo struck him so lightly. He thought of the rat he had seen splayed out on a chopping-board and the curiously ruined state of its intestines. Aloud he said, 'You bastard,' and the emerging rats shrank back.

There is a very big difference between dying for legitimate reasons, and dying because one's health has been dabbled about in by another. Ravel flung off his acceptance of his fate as if it were a hideous piece of apparel; his endorphins, task fulfilled, withdrew satisfied.

⟶

Did Ravel have any difficulty in believing what his logic was insisting – that Indigo, his beloved twin, was deliberately dosing him with rat poison? Not at all. Would you? On the contrary, he was elated by the realisation. He sat bolt upright and yelled. He'd reasoned out the final fact, and that fact proved the truth of everything that had gone before. He *wasn't* losing his mind, he'd been playing a *mind-game*. Ravel chortled with glee. He had won: he'd out-thought his wily twin. Indigo should have known better than to dice wits with *him*. His impulse was to jump from bed, rush down the stairs and throttle Indigo, but I advised caution. He was awfully weak by this time – after jumping from the bed he would only have flopped, embarrassingly, to the floor. He forgot, in his excitement, that his twin scorns repentance and is morally precarious. Fortunately I did not: I encouraged him to rest a while longer, to think his actions through, and he saw the wisdom and lay back down. He picked up a mug that was sitting on the floor and although the rats had licked it clean the walls of the vessel were tinged the faintest green, green like the box that contained the poison, green like the virulent pellets themselves. And green, of course, like peppermint milk.

Ravel had been right. From the moment he'd sus-pected something was wrong, he had been right. He wasn't forgetting anything, his life was still packed neatly in its box. He hadn't lost any Mrs Giottos, he'd never given anyone a necklace. Money grew, it didn't shrink. Indigo had been choking him, like a vine around a tree. Ravel had been right. And that meant Indigo was mad.

Mental torture is one thing: there's an element of the scientific to it. Surreptitiously dosing someone with rat poison, however, is quite another thing. It is an act of madness.

Indigo had been mad, Ravel admitted, for a long time. Not quirky and a touch peculiar, but utterly off his trolley, and dangerously so. This truth did not have any mind-numbing effect on Ravel. He reasoned that he'd been living alongside the madness all his life, and there was no cause to suddenly find it alarming. He'd outfoxed his foxy brother once, and he could do it again.

I have given Ravel everything he'll need. He has the necessary intelligence, and if he looks he will find the courage too. I can't help him any more than I have done, so it's time for me to go.

⟶

Indigo leaned against the door frame. 'What is it now?'

'Come here,' Ravel enticed.

'Are you hungry? Do you want something to drink?'

'No,' said Ravel. 'Come in. I just want to talk to you.'

Indigo hesitated, and Ravel could feel himself inspected. He tried to look more convincingly needy. 'I get lonely in here, without you,' he said, and Indigo smiled. He shut the door and sat on the end of the bed. He hadn't washed, but had doused himself liberally with a scent. He had evidently grown bored with the cloak and now wore one of his father's business shirts, which was big on him. His slim tawny legs were scuffed with dirt and there was grass flecking his feet. What had he been doing, Ravel wondered: playing in the garden?

'So . . . Have you got a job yet?'

'Not yet. I've had plenty of offers, but I'm choosy.'

'You should be. Anyone would be lucky to have you.'

'Wouldn't they.' Indigo squeezed Ravel's toes. 'You're sounding well today. Maybe you're getting better.'

'Yes. Things seem . . . clearer.'

'I think you've been ill for longer than either of us guessed. I think you were sick when you began getting those strange ideas.'

'Strange ideas? About going back to university? About getting a job?'

'Them.'

'But you're getting a job, now.'

106

'It's better that way. What's strange for you is sensible for me.'

'I see.' Ravel shifted under his sheet, slipping his foot from Indigo's grip. Indigo's touch would bruise him, and he needed his feet to work.

'I'll bring you some lunch soon.'

'Ah,' said Ravel. 'Goody.'

'It's hot again. I mean, it's an inferno out there.'

'Could you pass me the book?' asked Ravel. 'I want to read you a story.'

'I really haven't the time –'

'Please. It's the last story I'll read, I promise. It's a good one. You'll like it.'

Indigo yawned elaborately, showing all his teeth, and batted over the book.

———

Joseph Samuels pleaded guilty and was accordingly charged with the crime of breaking and entering the house of one Mary Breeze on August 25th, 1803. He was found to have taken from the house a writing-desk in which were locked 50 Dollars, 3 Guineas, 2 pieces of Gold Coin and assorted sundry articles. On the day following the crime, Constable Joseph Luker was brutally assassinated whilst trying to recover said desk from the haunt of a well-known gang. Samuels, by his own admission a member of this gang, was sentenced to hang.

The prisoner conducted himself with becoming decency throughout the trial. On the morning he was to die he was grilled for a final time on the matter of Luker's death. Samuels surprised his listeners by confiding that, while awaiting trial and sharing a cell with another member of the gang, Isaac Simmonds, he and Simmonds had entered a pact that would hold them to secrecy no matter what claims were made against them.

However, Samuels was a man preparing, now, to meet his Maker, and he wished to do so with no blotches upon his soul. Samuels swore that Simmonds, confident within the pact, had admitted to him (Samuels) that he (Simmonds) was responsible for the death of Constable Luker. Luker had discovered Simmonds while the villain was alone and hacking at the writing-desk: Simmonds had knocked Luker down, 'and given him a topper for luck!' It was a catastrophe that wasn't meant to happen but, Simmonds assured Samuels, he'd see five hundred innocents die before he danced from the gallows himself.

All this Samuels imparted with a stoic equability, his voice free of bitterness, much impressing those who heard him speak. Simmonds had avoided the death sentence through lack of evidence, but there were many who believed he was a guilty man. Simmonds's case was not helped when he took the news of Samuels's declaration somewhat badly. Great sympathy was extended towards Samuels, 'whose only probable concern it was to ease his burdened conscience', but this did not prevent him from stepping onto the cart from which he would be launched into eternity on the morning of September 26th, 1803.

Samuels had the noose placed around his neck and was allowed a minute of prayer before the cart drove away from beneath him. The prisoner hung suspended for only a moment before the rope snapped at its centre. Samuels, his hands and feet tied, fell promptly into the dust.

The rope was rewoven and the prisoner once more placed upon the cart. With a lash to the horses the cart trundled away, and the prisoner flailed the air. Then, remarkably, the rope began to unravel: what a ghastly, protracted, astonishing sight it must have been, watching Samuels descend painstakingly to the earth as the rope thinned itself out. Cries of Providence went up: there was a forgiving force at work here and perhaps it should be heeded. It was not: the other, less forgiving force demanded that Samuels, by now in all appearances lifeless, be hanged and hanged thoroughly. A fresh rope was thrown around the tree branch and once again they secured the prisoner by the neck.

They did not use the cart this time but chose the less abrupt method, that of hoisting the prisoner up bodily while the noose was placed at the throat. The men supporting the body were given the word and released their hold. The rope broke instantly.

The Provost-Marshal had had enough: he sped to the Court, related the story, and asked for a reprieve. This was granted, bringing relief to every horror-struck witness at the hanging ground. Samuels himself went on to regain his nerves and his health, but would never have clear recollection of the extraordinary events in which the main role had been his.

'They tested the rope later,' Ravel told Indigo. 'They hung a four-hundred-pound weight from it, and it held. There was nothing wrong with their *technique*, you see. It just wasn't going to work.'

'And the point is?'

'No point. I don't want points any more. I'm just telling you that punishment doesn't always work. You're stupid to think it will work.'

Indigo was sitting very still. 'You've got a bee in your bonnet about this punishment thing, haven't you,' he said.

'I seem to, yeah. I've been thinking about it a lot, these last few days.'

'Well, it's annoying me. I wish you wouldn't do that. You're not well. You're very vulnerable, lying there.'

'I am, aren't I?' Ravel was still feeling cocky and brave.

'If I annoy you too much, you might stop bringing me toast and milk.'

'If I wanted you dead, starvation is not the method I would use.'

'Oh, no! Imagine how I'd whinge and whine before I finally shut up for good. I agree, there's more efficient options. You could, for instance, drown me in a barrel of wine. Now there's a method with a proud history, I believe princes have gone that way in the past...'

Ravel frowned, and looked critically at his brother.

'It would require strength, though, wouldn't it?' he said. 'I mean, I wouldn't go down willingly, and you and I would be fairly equal in a test of muscle. A determination to succeed might make you stronger; determination to live would surely give me a physical boost. So how would you do it, I wonder? How do you quieten something that doesn't wish to be silent? Surprise, that's what you'd use, and something else, not your strength but something that gave you power, something in your control...'

Indigo's black stare softened, and he smiled. 'I get it,' he said. 'You're talking about Annie and Kasbah, aren't you? You've been lying there, feverish and wandering, pondering the fate of Annie and Kasbah.'

Ravel paused. 'Annie and Kasbah,' he said cautiously. 'That's right.'

'You've returned to that old hobby-horse of yours, the dog going back and back to the bone. Poor Ravel. You've never quite squished the suspicion that I did something to them, have you? You've never said a word, never mentioned the subject out loud, but it's been chewing at you, hasn't it? What did naughty Indigo do that day, when he went back into the house? What really happened to Mummy and Dad?'

Ravel lay motionless beneath his grubby sheet. 'Well,' he said, 'tell me.'

'What do you think happened?'

'They're dead, aren't they?'

Indigo looked surprised. 'That's a bit extreme, isn't it? Do you really think I snuffed my own parents? Ravel, I am deeply hurt.'

'I don't know what I think.'

'But you think they're dead. And I think so too.'

'How? What happened?'

'I don't know. But I'll tell you what I do know, if you like.'

'Please.'

Indigo settled against the wall, folding his hands in his lap. 'After I took you outside on that weird, wintry morning, I went back to the kitchen to talk to them. Annie was wailing like a banshee, as was her way, and I made Kasbah calm her down before I bothered to speak. When she managed to regain her senses, I explained that you appeared to have lost yours. Being in love, and being rejected. Humiliating for you, and understandably deranging. You needed care, and space, and delicate handling. You didn't need to be sent away, by yourself, to the other side of the globe. I suggested it would be easier if they went away instead, and left me in charge of the situation. Take a holiday, I said, go somewhere sunny and relaxing. You don't deserve this grief from your son. When you come home I'll have everything back to normal. Go for a month – go for two months, if you like.'

'And that's what they did, is it?'

'That's what they did.'

'Just packed up and left.'

'What else did they need to do? I rang the taxi that took them to the airport.'

'And you say they're dead, now.'

'It's a possibility. They've been gone a long time and without so much as a postcard. They could have had an accident in a foreign country. They could have rolled a car into a ditch, or been blown off the edge of a cliff, or been caught in a mudslide or a hurricane. There's a whole range of mishaps with the potential to carry them off. Perhaps they were murdered. You'd be surprised at the number of murderers out there. If something dastardly did happen, there might have been nothing left to identify them. A murderer would steal a passport. A fire would destroy luggage labels. We've made no enquiries after them, so they remain unclaimed.' Indigo smiled. 'Pauper's graves,' he added. 'My hands are quite clean.'

'You're a liar, Indigo.'

Indigo cocked his head and looked at his twin.

'You're lying. I don't think that's what happened.'

Indigo seemed unperturbed. 'Don't you?' he asked. 'Why is that? It all sounds plausible to me.'

'They wouldn't have left without saying goodbye to me.'

'But they *did*, didn't they? They left without saying goodbye to you.'

'Tell me the *truth*, Indigo!'

'The truth, Rav? The truth is that they didn't like you. They didn't want you. You were an *error*. There's one other reason why they haven't come back and that's because they don't *want* to come back. They don't want to see you *ever again*. And I'm beginning to agree with them. I'm sick of you, Ravel. I'm sick of your creepy shadow dragging after me. I'm tired of trying to make something worthwhile of you. You've never been worth the effort. You're a poor imitation. You've taken everything from me, but you only live because I do. You've leeched from me for years, and now I'm drawing the line. Blood-sucker. Hyena. Replica.'

Indigo climbed off the bed and walked from the room. Ravel slumped against his pillow, slick with sweat, frayed with shock. He'd trusted that brotherly affection would always keep him safe, hauling him back from the brink every time, but Indigo's affection had withered; it was gossamer. Indigo had *leapt* that brink and landed, unshackled, on the other side. He was mad, and suddenly there was nothing funny or familiar about that.

The door swung open with such force that it hit the wall and bounced shut again. Indigo strode across the floor and stopped before the bed. He had a large book under his arm, and he dropped it on Ravel's head. 'I'm bored with your stories,' he declared. He was swaying, a wrathful wraith. 'I've found a new book. It's a much better book. I'm going to read you something, but we'll get rid of this first, shall we?'

He scooped up Ravel's book of tales, yanked back the curtain, and sent the volume crashing through the window. Ravel ducked for protection from the light and the noise and the exploding glass, jamming himself against the wall.

The new book was *The Guinness Book of Records*. It was an old copy, out-of-date and grazed into holes by moths. It would leave a blue bruise on Ravel's left temple. Indigo flipped roughly through it until he found the record he wanted. *Pregnancy: Longest and Shortest.*

———

Calcification is the process by which matter is hardened by the depositing of calcium salts. Calcium is a malleable but durable metal, and, as calcite, is found in such solids as marble, limestone, eggshells and pearls. It is also found in some foodstuffs and in the bones and teeth of living

113

creatures. It is not surprising, then, that calcium and the process of calcification should feature in the account of the World's Longest Pregnancy.

In 1961 a Burmese woman was delivered by caesarean section of a baby weighing 1.3 kilograms (3 pounds). This woman had gone into labour in 1936 but no child had been born at that time. Twenty-five years of pregnancy had resulted in the calcification of the infant, and calcium, naturally a silver-white, turns yellow when exposed to oxygen. A perfect statue of a baby, then, hard as rock, rapidly shading from silver to yellow as the doctors looked on in amazement.

———

Ravel, cringing by the wall, looked at his twin with confusion. Indigo tossed aside the book and sneered down at him.

'A thousand points,' he said. 'The game is *over*.'

He stalked around the room, agitated, knocking treasures off the shelves. 'God,' he whined, 'I wanted so little from you. Just a touch of faithfulness. I have been trying – I have tried all my life – to find a touch of faithfulness. I only wanted it from the people who could give it easily: my parents, my brother. But no. It has always been too much to ask. I hate it, that the tiny thing I needed is more than anyone would give me. They didn't care for me. And now *you* want to leave.'

He stopped, his back to Ravel. 'Am I being melodramatic?' he enquired. 'Forgive me if I am. Melodrama is always mocked, isn't it? I don't know why. It means well. If I appeal strongly to your emotions, it is because I feel strongly emotional about the matter. And I do.'

He started walking again. 'You know what it's like not to be loved, Ravel,' he said. 'Remember how your heart broke? It got chewed up and spat out. You might have understood, because of that, but you don't. And I know why. It's because you're stone. You are, inside. You've a soul of cement. You're cold, like marble. I wish they'd left you inside Annie for twenty-five years – I wish you'd never been there in the first place. I can't bear the thought of your freezing hands touching me.'

He fell silent and gazed around the bedroom, chewing his lip with his teeth. He looked at the glass that littered Ravel's bed and at the curtain that bumped against the breeze. Finally he sniffed and said, 'You're not my real twin, anyway. Annie and Kasbah never told you, but they knew – the three of us knew. You remember, when we were kids, how they'd stare and stare at other children? That's who they were looking for. My *real* twin. My real twin is somewhere else, in some other shape. My real twin wouldn't call me a liar. He wouldn't get bored and hurt my feelings. He wouldn't want to leave me by myself. No, my real twin is good. He's kind. I want my real twin, Ravel. I'm just about done with you.'

Indigo spun on his heels and stalked out, closing the door after him. Ravel, watching him go, felt an insane desire to giggle. Terror has limits, like any other emotion, and when it reaches its peak it must change its essence or risk destroying the form it inhabits. For Ravel, everything changed from monstrous to absurd: he craved to screech with laughter. And laugh he would have, had not something distracted him. He heard a sound, a sound he didn't hear very often, but a sound he nonetheless recognised. It was unmistakably the sound of a bolt sliding home, as Indigo locked him in.

SMART, BUT NOT THAT SMART

Ravel was sitting on his bed, contemplating the glass spread over the floor. He sat as his mother had taught him to sit: chest out, head up, shoulders back. It was a haughty pose, and the twins had been teased for it at school. Children use horrible words against each other, they conjure horrible images. The twins kept their steady, regal disdain for them, for years.

Only Ravel's eyes drooped: they must, or else he could not see the glass. There was not very much glass – most of it had been thrown outwards, along with the book – but there was enough to create a small work of art. He'd gathered the pieces into a pile and laid them on his rug and then carefully arranged them so their skewed edges overlapped in some places and scarcely touched in others. To Ravel, the effect was mesmerisingly beautiful. The glass, and the faded blue carpet that was visible beneath it, reminded him of his dream. No – Indigo's dream. Ice.

He wanted to fall through ice and feel his body freeze, and if he could have that one wish granted he'd never ask for another thing.

Ravel was dying of thirst. If he pinched a fold of flesh on his arm the fold stayed standing for a long time, a flag, a sand dune, a sail. Four days had passed ponderously, the hours like molasses. The nights had gone more quickly, although he woke many times. The curtain was a shroud over what was once a window, and it wavered over empty space. In some hours Ravel would escape from here, while he was able, before he grew sicker still. He was waiting until nightfall, though he suspected Indigo didn't sleep.

The lock he'd fixed on his brother's door had presented Indigo with a problem during the first two days of Ravel's captivity. When he opened it to slide food into the room, he risked having the door wrenched from him and being overpowered before he recovered from the surprise. Ravel was capable of such deviousness. So Indigo put his trust in intimidation: he would loudly forewarn his twin that he was about to open the door, explaining that any attempt to escape would be met with a smart crack of the walking-stick he carried. He brandished this stick at his brother, to show he meant business. Ravel watched him but said nothing, and made no move to get from his bed.

On the third day Indigo abandoned the walking-stick as unnecessary. Ravel did not attempt to flee. Ravel seemed to do nothing at all. Morning and evening Indigo would find him in the same place, propped in the angle of the bed and the wall. He did not speak or twitch or yawn. He did not brush the flies that spooled the air before his face. If he had not blinked occasionally, Indigo might have thought Ravel was dead.

They never exchanged a word. Ravel simply watched, his gaze dulled with lethargy. And Indigo had nothing left to say to his twin: their long acquaintance was ended. He continued to bring toast and milk three times daily, but

117

he made no comment when he realised Ravel wasn't the one eating it.

───

It was a big walking-stick, stained unpleasantly dark, and its handle was fashioned into a duck's head. The duck had luminous yellow beads for eyes. It was a relic without a past, and the twins had used it when they were little and played dress-up. Indigo could not have imagined the effect the sight of it would have on Ravel.

Ravel had once been afraid of Indigo. It had been a complex fear, made of pieces like a jigsaw. Its central piece was placed the day his parents disappeared, and the rest of the pieces connected easily from there. Indigo had done something to Annie and Kasbah and it was frightening to wonder what. It was nerve-racking to live with the perpetrator of such a mystery. So Ravel had bowed to Indigo's insistence that the mystery never be mentioned, that he should become reclusive, because it was easy and *safest* to obey. Indigo, after all, was practised.

But Ravel's fear had reached its peak and changed its essence. It had broken into giggles, and it had kept on changing. He was locked in his room and he was wasting away, yet Ravel felt nothing but pity for his twin. He sorrowed for him, for the end of everything, and it was a relief when Indigo abandoned his weaponry because Ravel had never seen a more heart-rending sight than poor Indigo, fending off his brother's unforthcoming physical assaults with that pathetic walking-stick.

On the fourth morning Indigo sprinkled salt on the greasy surface of the toast.

───

At first the rats swooped upon the food as if they'd never eaten in their lives. The smartest were smart indeed: having figured out the new living arrangement between the brothers, they'd be waiting at the door as Indigo made his way to it. The biggest and most dominant would pounce upon the meal and consume it in moments. They'd fight over the toast, shouldering and snarling each other aside. They'd put their paws on the rim of the glass and speedily lick lick lick at the peppermint milk. When the level dropped beyond the reach of their tongues they'd use their weight to unbalance the glass so the milk ran over the floor and into the cracks between the boards. Lick lick lick, until it was gone. Smart, but not that smart.

The biggest, most dominant rats died first. They suddenly lost their appetite, realising too late that something was amiss. Their eyes took on an introspective glaze. They would sit as still as their jostling brethren allowed. Their suffering was painful for Ravel to see: it was better when they finally died.

On the third morning there were twelve dead rats in the room. Ravel gathered them up and threw them out the window, sending them as far as he could make them fly. The rats that survived – the smaller, younger, ineffectual rats – had seen what was happening and begun to grow wary. When Indigo opened the door that evening, none were there to greet him.

✦

If Ravel was stone he was volcanic stone, parched through, with gaping pores. He propped his elbows on the windowsill and scanned the sky for rain. If it rained he could collect the water in a glass, and then he could have a drink. At night he thought he heard the monumental gathering of storms, and saw white lightning gash across his eyelids; in the morning there were garbage trucks and the unbroken weight of the drought.

He heard Indigo in the house, the stomping and the clattering that he was supposed to hear. He detected also the sounds that Indigo wished to go unheard – the opening of the front door, the ear pressed against the bedroom door. He heard the shower of rust that fell from the staircase when Indigo climbed the steps to the tower, and he heard the trapdoor heave open. Indigo spent a long time in the tower and Ravel grew irritated, feeling his dominion being erased. Indigo would breathe in that musty air and breathe it out as his own. Ravel curled a fist to hammer on the wall – and unfurled it, knowing this was what Indigo was listening for.

The moment Indigo drove home the bolt had marked the beginning of an interesting game. Ravel saw it in his mind as a three-legged race, but one in which the partners were bound facing opposite directions, and gaining ground in one direction meant a frustrating loss of it in the other. If he did not eat and drink, he would no longer be dosed with green poison: this was one direction. But if he did not eat and drink, he would grow delicate indeed: the other direction. The tied-up partners battled it out, yearning to cross their opposing finishing-lines. For three days Ravel was a bemused spectator to this outlandish game. Poison, unsustained, was losing, and Ravel watched as the symptoms of warfarin were overtaken, in that tight little oven of a room, by those of dehydration.

He wasn't hungry: in four days he'd been untroubled by starvation. People don't often die of starvation – they die of diseases that take advantage of the cumulative, undermining effects of malnutrition. It tickled Ravel that he could remember details such as this, things he'd been taught or heard long ago. He declined to eat the toast for fear of what might be in it and he entertained himself with the possibilities – cyanide whipped into butter, perhaps, or arsenic powdered onto the crust. His stomach accepted emptiness with surprising good grace, and he understood that his body was once again his ally. Ravel would close his eyes and imagine the gluggy pools of poison that were gathered in his kidneys and liver and spleen. He willed the toxin out through the pores of his skin. He stood at the window and smiled to piss it goodbye.

On the ground directly below his window there was another work of art. It had taken Ravel some time to realise what it was, for his view from above was distorting. What he could see from his window was stakes. Indigo had planted a field of tall garden stakes. They were congregated close to the house, like triffids, the closest dug in flush to the wall. When a breeze blew they rapped against the wood. If Ravel had been inclined to jump from his third-floor bedroom he would have landed, unavoidably, upon them.

His bruises turned yellow, a shade lighter than his skin. There was seductive pain in pressing his thumbs into them, and he did this time and time again.

The human body is almost 70% water: to the human body, water ranks alongside oxygen in importance. We take in water through fluids and through solids, many of which contain a good deal of liquid. The quantity of water needed daily varies depending on circumstances, but the average grown body under average conditions needs approximately 2500 millilitres.

In hot conditions, such as Ravel was enduring, the amount of fluid lost through perspiration greatly accelerates the onset of dehydration. As the body sweats to cool itself it inadvertently dries itself out. The body tries to compensate for this by reducing the amount of water that passes through the kidneys, and one of the first symptoms of dehydration is a notable decrease in the amount, but sharp increase in the concentration, of urine. If the condition is not addressed, acute renal failure occurs. Waste products begin to collect in the system, and the result of this can be fatal.

Salt plays an interesting, somewhat duplicit role in dehydration. Salt creates a dryness in the mouth, causing thirst. But salt is vital to the correct functioning of the body, and salt, along with water, is lost through perspiration. When the salt level begins to drop, the body begins to crave.

Ravel thought the toast was coated with sugar, and he hurried to this glittering prize. Without knowing it, he began to cry: sugar, sweet and humble, meant Indigo was merciful, and Ravel was free. He rescued a slice from the rats and took a bite and that reminded him of all he'd fleetingly forgotten. He spat the food out and stared at it, for a moment grossly offended. He blinked and pouted and recomposed himself, and sighed.

His body yearned for salt, but if he ate salt he would become thirsty, and the only thing to drink was peppermint milk. Ravel didn't know he was crying, and he didn't know that he stopped. He rocked upon his haunches and his tired eyes considered the room. The rats looked back at him solemnly: they seemed to understand. They understood that soon they could eat *him*. Ravel understood that he was dying and that soon he would cross the line that marked the debilitation of no return. Indigo was not going to change his mind, and Ravel must act while he still possessed a mind that worked at all.

⤙

The four main compass directions are up, sideways, down, and sideways again. Down was not an option: Ravel, unlike the rats, could not drill through the floor, and down to the ground would offer no safe landing amongst the rattling stakes. To his left was an impenetrable wall and on his right was a wall that had been made impenetrable when Indigo attached a bolt to the door. An escape would need to reach upwards, as the trees grow.

He took the sheets from his bed and painstakingly ripped them into strips. He plaited the strips until they made a stringy rope. He measured the length of the rope carefully, laying it out across the room. He could afford to fall one floor, no further. He tied one end to a leg of his bed, just as he'd seen in the movies, and then he sat down to wait for darkness. He did not let himself think too closely on his plan, for thinking will always unearth holes.

It had been dark for hours when he took a hard-heeled shoe and battered out what remained of the glass in the window. This done, he tied the rope into a harness across his chest. Falling would wrench the air from him and leave him suspended like a ludicrous mobile, kicking feebly at the side of the house, but if his calculations were correct he would not fall as far as the points of the stakes.

Ready now, he took a final glance around the room. He had been in it for what felt like years, and leaving was suddenly intimidating. Out there, what would happen? Where would he go? He had no intention of abandoning Indigo, but Indigo would have to be given up. Indigo needed help and he would get it, although the walls of his new home would probably be padded. And Ravel would be free, but he would be alone, untwinned, born a second time but singular. Ravel could not imagine a life where his shadow did not breathe. He paused, gripping the curtain, resisting the force that was driving him out. The world beyond the house was an alien place to him: he didn't know what had been invented and discussed and discovered. He didn't know what had toppled or been resurrected. He knew nothing; he'd been left behind. Were certain things still wrong things and certain things right? Would he make mistakes and would people stare at him? Would he find the food inedible? Would it be, he wondered wildly, like the Planet of the Apes? He looked for something that might anchor him in the room forever, and saw the lock of hair that Indigo had offered as proof of a girl. It was banded by its ribbon and turning circles with the breeze, round and round and round. It would not stop spinning unless the wind dropped or grew strong enough to chase it from its place. Ravel stepped up to the windowsill.

The roof of his bedroom was beyond his reach, but not by much. The difficulty lay in negotiating the wide stretch of the eaves. He'd need to lean backwards into space for the shortest moment, trusting his umbilical cord of cotton sheeting, trusting that gravity can be cheated if you want to cheat it badly enough. A moment only (and who can remember every moment of a life?) when he must release his hold on the window frame and fling both arms up and outwards, and leap for the gutter on the spring of his legs. A moment there and gone, a moment of cursing Heaven and Hell and Annie and Kasbah and Indigo and himself, a moment in which to think nothing lest the holes in the plan make themselves loudly known and he'd plunge, ribs snapping as the rope yanked tight, and plunge further because the rope only worked in movies on the television he hadn't watched for ages because Indigo decided, Indigo decided everything including whether Ravel should live or die, and the sound of himself hitting those stakes would be the last thing he'd ever hear and what a ghastly sodden hideous sound that would be –

– so he let go, and jumped.

His fingers clamped around the gutter and Ravel,

terrified and in pain, hung there for some seconds, high above the ground. He whimpered and shifted his fingers, felt the guttering ease under his weight. He couldn't do this. At school he couldn't climb ropes. He would hit the stakes backwards and there'd be splinters in his spine. His boots scuffed the weatherboard and the paint flaked away. He inched himself up laboriously, carved his fingernails into the tiles, and when his chin was above the guttering he saw a smeared grainy light like a halo over the house. It came from the streetlamp: to Ravel it looked like life itself. He brought up a knee, found purchase, and swung onto the roof. He lay on his stomach for a long while, exhausted and traumatised but in victory, sweat cooling on his back as the warmth of the house infiltrated his chest.

Finally he rolled over, the cord trailing from him slackly, and smiled up at the stars. The Milky Way is our galaxy, but it is only one of billions. It is ten thousand light-years thick in its centre and one hundred thousand light-years in diameter. Within Milky Way's spiralling, dusty, gaseous arms float some hundred billion stars. These come in many types, among them the giant red stars and the brilliant blue stars, which include the super-giants. The stars began evolving more than five billion years ago and some are still being born today. The biggest star known has a diameter over five hundred times bigger than the sun's. The interior temperature of the average star is thirty to forty million degrees Fahrenheit.

The stars are made insignificant by the moon – our moon, the moon with no name. A quarter of Earth's size, lighter and trimmer in every respect, the moon has no running water and no breathable atmosphere; it has no weather, so its topography does not change. We see only half of it, and occasionally a sliver more.

The moon is made of gazes. The gazes are of awe,

of appreciation, and of fondness, the finest gazes that are given. Those we have loved, or lost, or missed because we were born too late or too soon or just too wrong, have all lifted their eyes to the moon. And because it has always been the same moon, we can look at it and know we're seeing something, admiring something, that the one we long for has also seen and admired, and we share something for a moment there, we almost touch . . . and this is comforting.

All this twinkled down on Ravel. 'Who's the king of the castle now, Indi?' he asked.

———

Indigo Kesby opened his eyes. He was lying on the floor of the dining-room, underneath the table. He'd been dozing and wondered what had woken him. He lifted his chin and yawned, like a lion, and nestled his head in the crook of his arm.

———

Slabs of roofing made Ravel feel like an angel, or Batman. He skimmed lightly from one plane to another, up and down, back and forth. He remembered that the house was a tale-telling creature, as willing as a righteous child to report the goings-on, so he stopped to remove his boots. He didn't feel ill and frightened any more – he was exultant, drunk with his escape. He stumbled once or twice, for the tiles were loose and badly warped, but he pushed himself up and hurried on, swerving past the chimneys with his sights on the ground.

At the tower he paused to catch his breath, resting his forehead against the glass. He closed his eyes and remembered the danger he was in, and opened his eyes again. The tower, lit by moonlight, was messy inside. Ravel wiped the window and looked closer. Curiosity kills cats and it could kill him, but for the moment he felt safe – safer than he would be once he touched the earth. He tugged open a window and slipped through the spiderwebbed gap, into the octagonal room. There was a lock on the tower's trapdoor and the first thing he did was click it closed. He crouched, then, amidst the mess, and whistled through his teeth.

Indigo had brought the family albums here, but not to reminisce. He'd taken the photographs from each of them and pushed the empty albums aside. He'd been concerned only with photos that depicted his brother and himself; the rest, including the ones of Annie and Kasbah, had been balled up and thrown into a corner. He'd made two untidy piles out of photographs of the twins and Ravel rifled through them, peering through the gloom.

One pile was him, and the other pile was Indigo. Some photos, the ones that pictured Indigo and himself together, had by necessity been cut in two. The cuts were surgically neat. Annie's writing, on the back of these cleaved photographs, read *Twi* and *Twins age* and *ins aged four*. Ravel touched the letters, remnants of his lazy and confused mother. It suddenly seemed an infinitely sad, infinitely trivial thing, that she couldn't distinguish one twin from the other. What had it mattered? Worse has been done, and is done all the time. He looked at the photographs, the two piles kept well away from each other, the images cleanly severed, and felt he could weep. He stared at himself as a little boy and knew the child would not recognise him. Like all children he had hoped for the best, and nothing had turned out the best way it could. He did not think this dark-haired child would forgive him for the things that had been allowed to happen.

Only – the child wasn't him. Ravel frowned, suddenly sure of it. He'd taken the photograph from his own pile

127

and the photograph was not of him. It was Indigo. Indi had made a mistake. Ravel skimmed through the photographs, holding them up one after another to the light of the moon. Indigo had mistaken himself five, six, seven times. The differences that glared so obviously to Ravel evidently did not always catch Indigo's attention. That, to Ravel, was bitterly amusing.

He selected two photographs, his favourites, one of Indigo and one of himself, and slipped them into his pocket. From the pile of crumpled discards he took the first photo of his parents that he found. He smoothed it flat and tucked it away and then he climbed out the window into the darkness. He had lost time and he would hurry now, he would not stop.

Along the rooftop he flitted, a phantom with dimensions. He struggled to be silent and he wasn't: eyes flipped open to watch him, ears turned like radars to track him as he went. Cats saw him and were distracted from their heckling of each other; dogs saw him and began to howl, ruffled by the sight.

———◆———

Under the dining-room table Indigo jerked a leg stiffly, and stubbed a toe against a chair. He woke grizzling with the pain of it, and rubbed his face with the back of his hand. He pricked his ears and opened his eyes. Dogs he could hear, and something else.

———◆———

Ravel dropped off the kitchen porch and into the back garden. The drop jarred him, yanked the energy out of him, and he slouched forward on his palms. He stayed down, his mind reeling, his body shivering. The garden tap was close and he wondered if water would react within him violently now, making him sick or making him faint. The prospect was upsetting: he thought his frame could not endure another strike against it. Equally, he could not crouch in the darkness indefinitely, waiting for Indigo to find him. His hands seemed impacted into the concrete of the footpath and he lifted them with a heavy effort.

He reached the tap and turned it on, gently, so the water came out in a wiggling stream. Ravel cupped his hands and looked into them, dry and empty, before he ducked the cup under the stream and waited for it to overflow.

———

Water covers three-quarters of our planet, and it does so with a vengeance. The oceans are, on average, more than five times as deep as the continents are high. Most of the water is undrinkable, although science has occupied itself in finding methods of making this otherwise, in an effort to meet the ever-growing demand for fresh fluid. What water we can drink we purify, chlorify, and soften to our taste. Water contains fluorides, and these are good for our teeth. Water is a favourite weapon for lunatics who would attempt to wipe out great numbers of the population in a single throw. Water is what we are, and water is relatively cheap. Buying the water inside ourselves would cost less than a dollar.

The first mouthful made him splutter, but Ravel persisted. He drank until the thought of drinking made him gag. He doused his head, his greasy hair, and wiped down his arms and legs. The earth beneath the tap became muddy, and so did he.

There was no time to linger. He would come back, but everything depended on the success of his escape, and before he could return for Indigo he needed to get as far from him as possible. Without money, he had no idea where he'd go. He needed food, and wondered where he'd get it. A hospital, perhaps. He was a good candidate for a cosy bed in a hospital.

He turned to go, and glimpsed the face looking out at him. For a second his heart stopped, his blood chilled, for he thought the face belonged to Indigo. It was a tiny face, a suggestion of a face peeping through a window of the underground, watching him between the stalks of rigid weeds. It retreated into the darkness when he caught its eye and the word that came to Ravel's mind was *stricken*. The face was stricken: it was stricken at seeing him, stricken at being seen, and it definitely didn't belong to Indigo.

Ravel hesitated. He spun to go and spun around again. He didn't want to know who was in the room, he didn't want to know why the creature was there and what was being done to it. He wanted to run away. He stamped his feet and scratched his face with frustration. He felt a hatred for the face and its owner, derision for its obvious fear. He hated it because now he had to go inside and he didn't want to go inside, he was frightened of going inside. He was frightened of Indigo, and he hated Indigo too. Indigo had reduced him to a tentative, tiptoeing, home-less, impoverished, isolated and embittered – *wretch*. Ravel swore, and stormed back and forth, and kicked peevishly at the grass.

But – Ravel, listen – wouldn't Indigo be furious if all his toys were taken away from him? Ravel found the courage, and swept back his hair.

⌐⌐

The Piper came to Hamelin because the place was riddled with rats and no one but he could do anything about it. He came dressed beautifully in a pied red and yellow cloak and he carried a silver flute. He set his price at a thousand guilders and the desperate townsfolk readily agreed.

The Piper played a tune that spoke to the rats. It spoke of delectable foods, of free-flowing garbage, of a land where no cats or traps existed. The rats, entranced, followed the tune to this wondrous land. One by one they found themselves plunging into the river and being washed away.

The Piper returned to Hamelin to collect his thousand guilders but the people had grown suddenly churlish. They did not see why they should pay for something already so securely done, and they told the Piper to get on his way. The Piper's face grew sad and angry. He lifted the flute to his downturned lips and the notes rang sweet and clear. From every nook in Hamelin, a child came running. The children heard, in the tune the Piper played, the promise of a better world, where difference was not derided, where streets were safe to play in, where injections were unnecessary, where school holidays never came to an end.

The people stood frozen, watching their children dance away. The Piper led them to a mountain and the mountainside opened up. The Piper and the children went through this doorway and the mountain rumbled closed behind them. Neither the Piper, nor the children, were ever seen again.

This is what they call a *fairy-tale*.

The corridors were dark and Ravel wasn't sure of his way. Several times he stopped to listen, raising his eyes to the pitch ceiling of the underground. He listened for footsteps above him, and scanned the blackness before and behind him. There were places for Indigo to hide down here, fireplaces and stairwells and deep alcoves. There were tunnels that slithered away to surface inside and outside the house. There were secret doors and connecting doors and doors swollen shut. Ravel listened, heard nothing, lurched onwards.

❦

Indigo turned a circle across the floor, his arms outspread. Like the needle of a compass he turned, tracing direction, his fingertips tapping air, tapping noise. His bare feet slid gracefully over the silky carpet, treading soundlessly on sound. Vibrations shimmered through his ankles and up the back of his calves and finally Indigo stopped spinning. He dropped a hand and his fingers pointed downwards, pinning the sound like a butterfly.

❦

Ravel fumbled with the bolt on the door, a twin to the bolt on his bedroom door, equally shiny and new. It was not padlocked but it had been driven home hard. His muscles, drained by all they'd been put through, struggled with the heavy wand of metal, and when it shot back unexpectedly Ravel staggered sideways, his knuckles smacking the plastered walls.

He opened the door widely, rashly. At first he saw nothing but the seams of the room, the shadows darker here than anywhere. And then a boy stepped into his line of vision and, seeing him, Ravel understood it all. A boy of strange resemblance to himself, imperfect resemblance but resemblance enough. Indigo had found his lost twin. He'd played a tune that was irresistible, and the mountainside had opened up. The boy's face was stony, and in his fist he held a length of piping that he had ripped from the ancient water system.

'Wait,' said Ravel, and his hands came up to save himself. 'I'm not Indigo, I'm not Indigo –'

The boy, deaf with his momentum, swung the piping, and whacked Ravel across the face.

❦

A peculiar rasping noise woke him and Ravel opened his eyes. He lay crumpled in a corner and a draught was blowing in on him, the cold wet air of the underground. The rasping sound was coming from himself: it was the sound of his breathing. His teeth had broken and blood was clogging his mouth. He pushed himself to his elbows and spat the blood on the floor. Did it look especially thinned, that blood? In the darkness he couldn't tell.

He lifted his head and blinked groggily. Indigo was standing before him, his hands on his hips. He sought to catch his brother's eye but Ravel glanced instead around the room. He couldn't see the boy and hoped he was safely gone, hoped he had successfully navigated the maze of rooms and not disappeared forever.

'Well,' said Indigo. 'Well.'

Ravel looked sideways at him. He'd never get to his feet, he was completely finished. This corner was the corner he'd die in, and Indigo would leave him here, pausing only to rebolt the door. He looked at his brother for a silent moment, wondering what he should say. Protests and repentance and torrents of devotion would not even make a dent. Indigo was mad, mad as a hatter. Perhaps he was even madder. Perhaps there was no limit to how mad he was, or to the things he could do, or to the things he could be made to do.

Indigo had always said they were twins, and interchangeable. Indigo always said that a *name* was a fragile hook on which to hang an identity, that a name has less substance than air – but if your *face* is not even your own, what is? And if your *face* is not your own, who's to say *who* owns it?

'You've escaped from your room, I see.'

Words were cold in that chilly underground, and hit

the floor like icicles. Ravel's teeth clattered painfully and Indigo made no move.

'Very wicked of you.'

Ravel felt his heart start hectically pounding: it was a coward, and wanted to abandon his chest to its fate. His body longed to weep and wail and grovel on the floor. But his brain – his brain was a professional. It thought, and its thinking was crystalline.

'But that's all right. The game is over. You passed the test.'

Indigo finally moved: he flicked up an eyebrow. Ravel plucked out his words, talking for his life.

'I've been so bad, haven't I? I worried you sick.'

'Excuse me: what are you talking about?'

'You know ... you do know, don't you? You didn't believe it, did you? That stuff about the girl and the gas and everything – you never believed it, did you?'

Ravel glanced hopefully at his brother. He was praying. He was talking and inside he was praying. He was a scientist and an atheist, praying fervently to the god of the impossible.

'It was your own fault,' he said. 'You made me do it. What else could I do? You were going to leave me here by myself. Imagine how lonely I would have been! Imagine what a mess you would have made ...'

Ravel endeavoured to look grieved. Indigo gazed steadily back at him.

'So I had to *remind* you. Remind you that you need me, to keep you safe. And that I need you, and you shouldn't be mean to me ...'

It wasn't working. It was never going to work. He laughed.

'Mrs Giotto – she was cute, wasn't she? The speech impediment was a stroke of genius. It was a shame she was make-believe, I got quite fond of her. But she scared you, didn't she? Snooping around. That was funny. I'm sorry, Rav, but it was.'

'I'm not Ravel.' He sounded certain, and rather bored. Ravel rolled his eyes.

'God, one minute you want to be Ravel, the next minute you don't want to be. You're confused, aren't you? I'm not surprised. My intention was to confuse you, and you know I'm good at what I do. You didn't know what to make of that girl coming around, and that stupid lock of hair. Don't you remember telling me what she looked like? You used to tell me all the time. *Ooh Indi, she's gorgeous.* And she didn't sound like she was at all, you fibber. And that necklace – you should have seen your face –'

'Listen: *I'm* Indigo.'

Ravel took a deep breath.

'That's the sort of stubbornness that made me cross, Ravel. Every time I tried to be nice you'd do something to annoy me. We're not really running out of money. I only said it because you were driving me insane. What I mean is, the whole thing would have been over long ago if you hadn't been stubborn. Stubborn and stupid: you were.'

The twins shook their heads. Ravel kept his eyes on his beautiful brother, wondered if he had ever looked like that.

'So I had to poison you.'

The smile on Indigo's face suddenly slipped, and he could not catch it as it fell.

'I wasn't going to *kill* you. What do you think I am? Why would I do that, and leave myself alone? It wouldn't be consistent. I just wanted to imprint a little association on your brain – you know, like Pavlov's dog. You'd feel sick every time you thought about leaving me. And you do, don't you?'

135

Indigo, his face blank, remained silent.

'That kid – I'd have loved to see your face when you saw him wearing your clothes, playing with your treasures. He really would have rattled you. I wasn't going to keep him, of course. I would have let him go when he'd served his purpose.'

'You're *wrong.*'

'No, I would have, I promise.' Ravel paused, and looked contrite. 'Forgive me, Rav,' he said. 'It was all very childish. But I had to be sure. Faithfulness is important to me. And you overcame everything – your confusion, your pain – to stay with me. Look at you, look how sick and bashed up you are, but here you are. Why, you'd crawl over broken glass for me, wouldn't you? And that's what I call faithfulness.'

'I'm *Indigo –*'

'Yeah, you've always wanted to be, haven't you? It's flattering. And anyway, who is who? Look at this, look what I've got: who is who?'

He drew from his pocket the two photographs he'd taken from the tower. One picture was of Ravel and the other was of Indigo, but Indigo had mistaken both of them for himself. They were photos that had been scissored in half and their edges looked sharp. The effect that the sight of them had on Indigo was reassuring: he stepped back uneasily, as if his balance had tipped.

'We are twins,' said Ravel. 'Interchangeable. We are Ravel, you are Ravel. We are Indigo, I am Indigo. *I'm* Indigo, Ravel.'

Indigo's gaze darted from the photographs and brushed the length of himself. 'No,' he said, 'that's me.'

Ravel, back to the wall, yelped, 'For God's sake, will you stop! What do you want me to say? Do you want me to tell you what happened to Annie and Kasbah? Will that make you happy? Of course I did it. You *know* I did it. It was *easy*. They never knew what was happening. It didn't hurt. I used chemicals to quieten them – I've got bucket-loads of chemicals, you know. I used a bolt to shut them away. Bolts are very handy unless some spoilsport goes and opens them. And that's all, Ravel. They're not far from here but no, I'm not showing you where. I'll never show you where. And that's all.'

His twin hesitated. 'I'm Indigo,' he repeated, with failing certainty. 'I know I am.'

'I think I know more about me than you do, Ravel,' said Ravel nastily.

Indigo didn't answer, but he looked bereft. Madness is greedy: it takes everything, in the end. Once he had had two identities, and now he could put his name to none. Ravel felt no joy in his victory.

'. . . It's cold in here, Rav. I'm cold, and I'm hurt.'

Indigo glanced up through the saddest eyes. 'Your face,' he said. 'It's bleeding.'

'My teeth aren't straight any more.'

'We'll never look the same again.'

'No.' Ravel smiled wearily, and placed his hand in the tacky pool of blood. 'Help me up,' he said, 'and we'll get out of here. It's cold, and you're ill.'

'I'm not . . .'

'Yes. You've been drinking rat poison for a couple of weeks. Help me up. Now, Rav.'

Indigo extended a hand into the darkness and with his help Ravel got to his feet. He squeezed his brother's shoulder while he coughed out another mouthful of blood.

'Are you all right?'

'Yeah. Let's go outside.'

'Outside?'

'It's warm outside.'

137

'But it's night.'

'I know. But it's warm. And I don't feel like being in the house. Do you, Ravel?'

Indigo shrugged, as if he'd lost his words as well.

'Well,' said Ravel, 'I want to go outside. I want to look at the moon. And I want you to look at it too.'

'What for?'

'You'll know when you see it.'

Indigo nodded, and dutifully supported his brother, and together the Kesby twins made their way up from the black underground and into the shining garden. They stopped in a clearing of tendrils and weeds and Ravel lay down in its softness, too tired to stand any longer. Indigo folded to the earth awkwardly, assuming that this was what he was required to do.

The breeze had picked up, strong enough to flick their hair and dust their clothes and make the empty house whistle. The building was not their home any more and Ravel guessed its fate, the helpless inward tumbling, the final heaving groans. He had wanted change and, careless what he'd wished for, he'd received more changes than he had expected, but he would have courage, regret nothing, remember all. From down amongst the sagging weeds his eyes pursued the starry links of the sky until they reached the moon.

'Look,' he sighed. 'Look up there.'

Indigo looked up and saw the moon. The moon is majestic and singular, and it has fulfilled its task as collector of gazes for thousands and thousands of years, but on this night it failed. Indigo glanced at it and away; his eyes sought for his sleeping twin, and he reached out a hand.

NOTE

The author wishes to acknowledge the following sources:

Ingleton, G. C. (ed.), *True Patriots All*, Angus & Robertson, Sydney, 1952.

Llewellyn-Jones, D., *Everywoman: A gynaecological guide for life*, Penguin, Melbourne, 1993.

Nuland, S. B., *How We Die*, Chatto & Windus, London, 1994.

Page, M., and Ingpen, R., *Out of This World: The complete book of fantasy*, Lansdowne Press, 1986.

Toohey, M., *Medicine for Nurses*, E. & S. Livingstone, Edinburgh and London, 1960.

Weir, A., *The Princes in the Tower*, Arrow Books, London, 1995.

Encyclopaedia Britannica, Britannica Advanced Publishing, Chicago, 1996.

Funk & Wagnalls New Encyclopedia, Funk & Wagnalls, New York, 1973.

The Guinness Book of Records 1991, Guinness Publishing, 1990.